Parallel Worlds

Herbie Brennan is a professional writer whose work has appeared in more than fifty countries. He began a career in journalism at the age of eighteen and when he was twenty-four became the youngest newspaper editor in his native Ireland.

By his mid-twenties, he had published his first novel, an historical romance brought out by Doubleday in New York. At age thirty, he made the decision to devote his time to full-length works of fiction for both adults and children. Since then he has published more than a hundred books, many of them international bestsellers, for both adults and children.

Other books by Herbie Brennan
published by Faber and Faber

Space Quest
111 peculiar questions about the universe and beyond

The Ghosthunter's Handbook

The Aliens Handbook

The Codebreaker's Handbook

Herbie Brennan's Forbidden Truths: Atlantis

Herbie Brennan's Forbidden Truths: Time Travel

Herbie Brennan's Forbidden Truths: Strange Powers

HERBIE BRENNAN'S FORBIDDEN TRUTHS

Parallel Worlds

Illustrated by The Maltings Partnership

faber and faber

First published in 2007 by Faber and Faber Limited
3 Queen Square, London WC1N 3AU

Designed by Planet Creative, Andy Summers
Editorial Management: Paula Borton
Illustrated by The Maltings Partnership

Printed in England by Bookmarque Ltd

A CIP record for this book is available from the British Library

ISBN 978-0-517-22316-9

2 4 6 8 10 9 7 5 3 1

Contents

Chapter 1   A Teenager from Nowhere   9

Chapter 2   The Children from Nowhere   23

Chapter 3   Things from Nowhere   33

Chapter 4   Creatures from Nowhere   44

Chapter 5   Visitors from Nowhere   55

Chapter 6   Disappearing Things   67

Chapter 7   Disappearing People   78

Chapter 8   Mass Disappearances   92

Chapter 9   Einstein's Revolution   103

Chapter 10 The Impossible Experiment   111

Chapter 11 The Philadelphia Experiment   119

Chapter 12 Fairyland   128

Chapter 13 Real Fairies   135

Chapter 14 Megalithic Weirdness   154

Chapter 15 Megalithic Machine   160

Chapter 16 International Grid   171

Chapter 17 Here be Dragons   180

Afterword   193

For Paula, with a thousand thanks.

What if…

    … you can't trust your teachers? What if you can't believe your parents?

What if…

    … the things you know for sure are just plain wrong?

What if…

    … scientists sometimes just *make up* the answers?

What if...

... the world is not the way you think it is? What if physics is all lies? What if the stuff they tell you is impossible keeps happening every day?

What if...

... Fairyland actually exists?

Chapter 1
A Teenager
from Nowhere

The city of Ansbach sprawls beside the Rezat River some distance south west of Nuremberg in southern Germany. Benedictine monks began its building in AD 748. Today it contains a very odd memorial. In the *Hofgarten* park that surrounds Ansbach Castle there stands a lonely pillar with a brief, plain inscription. Should you have trouble with the Latin when you visit, I can tell you it translates as:

> At this place for mysterious reasons
> one mysterious figure was murdered
> by another mysterious figure.

The victim of the murder was called Kaspar Hauser. His headstone in Ansbach Cemetery carries another Latin inscription: *Hic jacet Casparus Hauser aenigma suit tempora ignota nativitas occulta mors.* That one translates as: Here lies Kaspar Hauser, riddle of our time, his birth unknown, his death mysterious.

Despite the air of mystery, a great deal is actually known about Kaspar Hauser. His story begins in Nuremberg on May 26, 1828. The day was Whit Monday and much of the city was deserted as its citizens took themselves off on holiday. One who stayed at home was a cobbler named George Weichmann. He was taking a stroll across the empty Unschlitt Square when he noticed a teenage boy lurching down the hill towards him.

The boy looked about 16 or 17 years of age and was sturdily built, but dressed in rags. What's more, he scarcely seemed able to speak. But he did mumble something under his breath as he handed Weichmann an envelope. Weichmann glanced down to discover it was addressed to 'The Captain of the 4th Squadron, 6th Cavalry Regiment in Nuremberg'.

Weichmann took the boy to the nearest military post, which happened to be the New

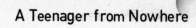

Gate Guardroom, and turned him over to the Sergeant-in-Charge. As it happened, the Sergeant knew the Captain of the 4th Squadron – his name was Wessenig – and directed the boy to where he lived. The Captain was out, but his servants told the boy he could wait.

Some hours later, Captain Wessenig came home to find his house in an uproar. The boy had been sick because of the smell of cooking from the kitchen, but wolfed down black bread and drank huge quantities of water. He was terrified when the grandfather clock struck the hour and wouldn't go near it when the servants tried to reassure him. Although beer is Germany's most popular drink, he not only refused some, but clearly had no idea what it was. Even more mysteriously, he had tried to pick up a candle flame between his fingers and roared with pain and astonishment when it burned him.

Captain Wessenig opened the envelope with his name on it. Inside were three pieces of paper, pinned together. First came a two-page letter, written in a florid, ornate style of Gothic German. The second was an 18-line note, rather more crudely composed. The handwriting appeared to be different, although in both, each line was carefully numbered. The letter was addressed to the 'High Well-born Captain' and unsigned. It read:

1   I send you a young man who wishes
2   to serve his King in the Army. He
3 was brought to me on October 7, 1812.
4 I am only a poor labourer with children of
5 my own to bring up. His mother asked me to
6 bring up this lad and so I thought I would
7 rear him as my own. Since then I have
8 never let him go one step outside the house,
9 therefore no-one knows where he was
10 reared. He himself does not know the name
11 of the place or where it is. You may question
12 him, Honourable Captain, but he will not
13 know where I live. I brought him out at
14 night. He will not be able to find his way
15 back. He has no money, for I have none
16 myself. If you will not keep him, you must
17 strike him dead or hang him.

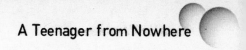

The attached note, dated October 1812, read simply:

> 1 this boy has been baptised his name
>
> 2 is kaspar you must give him his
>
> 3 second name yourself. i ask you to
>
> 4 take care of him his father was a
>
> 5 cavalry soldier when he is 17. take
>
> 6 him to nuremberg to the 6th cavalry
>
> 7 regiment his father belonged to it. i
>
> 8 beg you to keep him until he is 17.
>
> 9 he was born on april 30, 1812 i am a
>
> 10 poor maid i cannot take care of
>
> 11 him his father is dead

As the Captain read the letters aloud, young Kaspar became increasingly excited. It quickly became clear he could talk, but only after a fashion. He shouted 'horse... horse...' several times and repeated the phrase 'want to be a soldier like my father.' He was fascinated by the Captain's sabre and tried to stroke its handle. Wessenig quickly decided the boy was mentally defective and, anxious to avoid taking responsibility, marched him straight to the nearest police station.

Following established procedure, a policeman handed Kaspar paper and pencil and instructed him firmly to write down his name and address. Kaspar carefully scrawled the words 'Kaspar Hauser'.

'Now the address,' said the policeman. But Kaspar Hauser shook his head and said, '*Weiss nicht. Weiss nicht.*' ('Don't know. Don't know.')

A police sergeant named Wüst was called in. He later wrote a description of Kaspar Hauser that has survived to this day. According to the sergeant, he was a sturdy, broad-shouldered teenager with blue eyes and brown hair. He looked healthy, except for the fact that he seemed to be crippled. At first Wüst thought there must be something wrong with his legs, but closer examination showed the problem was his feet. The soles were so tender they had blistered from walking.

Kaspar was stripped and searched. None of his clothes seemed to fit him. His trousers and jacket were far too big as were his hat and his shirt. But his boots were far too small. There was nothing in his pockets except a rosary, a packet of salt and two religious texts of the sort that get given out on street corners.

The police next turned their attention to the letters and quickly concluded they were fakes. On the face of it they had been written 16 years ago, but the ink looked too fresh for that. Although one was written in a formal style and the other more roughly, both were on exactly the same sort of paper and the handwriting was similar enough to make Sergeant Wüst suspect the same person had penned the two. For some reason, somebody was trying to create a fictional background to the boy. Was it Kaspar himself? Apparently not, since his own childlike scrawl bore no resemblance to the writing on the letters.

All the same, the police locked him in a cell 'for further observation'. What they observed was bizarre. Young Kaspar clearly preferred the darkness to the light and could move around with the ease of a cat. Except that he didn't move around all that much. Instead he sat for hours immobile as a statue and didn't seem to sleep.

From time to time, his jailers would take him out and question him again, but without any breakthrough. Again and again he parroted the desire to become a cavalryman 'like his father' but beyond the German for boy, every question was answered 'I don't know.'

It soon became clear Kaspar Hauser was not at all like any teenage boy Nuremberg had ever seen. He looked normal enough – big, strong and healthy – but his reactions were those of somebody who'd just landed from another planet. Hand him a knife and he would take it by the blade, often cutting himself in the process. Hand him a watch and he would listen to the

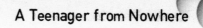

ticking for hours. He had no idea there was any difference between men and women: he called both *junge*, the German for boy. He couldn't tell the difference between various animals either: everything was a 'horse'. Dogs were horses, cats were horses, rats and mice were horses.

Somebody brought him a toy horse eventually, made from wood. Kaspar decorated it with ribbons and pretended to feed it every time he ate anything himself. There were all sorts of everyday things, like coins and playing cards, which he had obviously never seen before. Most amazing of all, he had absolutely no sense of personal privacy. When he needed the toilet, he calmly went on the floor, absolutely unconcerned that anyone was watching.

On the face of things, it seemed as if young Kaspar Hauser might be a simpleton, some poor, brain-damaged boy innocently making his way through the world as best he could. But this quickly proved not to be the case. From the standing start of his original appearance when he could barely scrawl his name, was unable to read at all and spoke fewer than a dozen words, he taught himself to read, write and speak fluently in just six weeks. And at the end of that time, he penned a fluent account of what had happened to him.

According to Kaspar, he had lived for as long as he could remember in a two-metre long darkened cell, 1.2 metres wide and 1.5 metres high. The window was boarded up, the floor was bare earth and there was a pile of straw for him to sleep on. He was never able to stand upright and he certainly could not walk. His only companions were three toy wooden horses.

Somebody brought him food while he slept, but only ever a loaf of black bread and a jug of water. From time to time the water would contain something that sent him into a particularly deep sleep. When he awoke at these times, he had fresh straw, his clothes were changed and his nails and hair had been cut. These were the only changes in his monotonous routine. There were no visitors, no outside sounds and the light level never varied.

Then one day a man entered the cell and placed a wooden board across Kaspar's knees. The man gave him pencil and paper, then painstakingly taught him how to write the words

Kaspar Hauser. The man also taught him how to repeat a few phrases like *Don't know* and *I want to be a soldier like my father*. Once the man stormed into his cell and hit him with a stick for making too much noise. But that was all there was until, after one of his deeply drugged sleeps, everything changed for Kaspar Hauser.

He woke to find that for the first time in his life he was wearing boots. His mysterious jailer entered the cell and led him out into the light. He was bewildered, dizzy, confused and could scarcely remember what happened to him except that he walked until his feet were sore and found himself at the gates of Nuremberg.

It was a story that caused a sensation. Visitors arrived from all over Germany to see the unfortunate boy. Kaspar was made a ward of the city. The municipal authorities issued thousands of handbills with his picture, offering a substantial reward for anybody who had information about his background. The Bavarian police mounted a search for the cell in which he'd been imprisoned.

None of it helped. Kaspar remained a mystery and quickly turned into an international tourist attraction. A renowned professor named Georg Friedrich Daumer was appointed his guardian and Kaspar became a celebrity, attending parties and entertaining curious members of the nobility.

But life proved to be not all a bed of roses and, following what appeared to be an attempt on his life, Kaspar was moved to Ansbach in the spring of 1883. By mid December he was dead. On the snowy Saturday afternoon of December 14, Kaspar staggered home bleeding from a wound in his side and claiming he'd been stabbed while walking in the Hofgarten by a tall man in a dark cloak who had handed him a silk purse.

A military officer assigned to Kaspar rushed to the Hofgarten and found no sign of the cloaked attacker, but did discover the silk purse. Inside

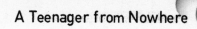

was a note in mirror writing, identifying the assailant as 'M.L.O.' and claiming he came from the Bavarian border. Kaspar died three days later. Despite the clues in the note, his murderer was never found.

> Hauser will be able to tell you how I look, whence I came from and to who I am. To spare him that task, I will tell you myself: I am from – On the Bavarian border – On the River – My name is M.L.O.

Kaspar Hauser's death was mysterious – the military officer discovered only one set of footprints where the purse was found – but then so was his entire life. Although repeated endlessly and eventually published in booklet form, the story he told about his origins was clearly nonsense.

To have spent his entire life in a lightless cell would have left Kaspar Hauser as pale as a corpse, yet all descriptions mention that he looked fit and healthy. It would also, according to the best medical opinion, have left him blind.

Parallel Worlds

No-one could survive for years on a diet of bread and water: if nothing else he would have been dead from scurvy in a matter of months (a disease caused by a lack of vitamin C when fruit and vegetables are not eaten). And anyone confined to a cell where he could neither walk nor stand would find their muscles wasting away over much the same period.

Yet while Professor Daumer did confirm the boy's eyes reacted badly to sunlight, he was far from blind and his vision functioned with startling efficiency in the dark. Furthermore, he had an extraordinary sense of smell, almost matching that of a dog.

So Kaspar emerged out of a gloomy somewhere, but there is no way he could have been confined to a darkened cell as he claimed. Which leaves the crucial question: where did Kaspar Hauser come from?

Chapter 2
The Children
from Nowhere

Perhaps Kaspar Hauser came from the same place as the green children of Woolpit. Today, Woolpit is a quiet, picturesque village in the English county of Suffolk, the sort of place where the pace of life is slow, nothing much happens and the residents very much like it that way. But more than 850 years ago, something happened in Woolpit that was so bizarre it is still written about and discussed to this day.

The actual date is a little uncertain, but best guess suggests it was in or around the year 1150, a period when King Stephen was on the throne of England. They were troubled times. It was only 11 years since Stephen had been forced to put down an armed revolt and even now, there were pockets of the country outside the King's control.

None of this very much affected a sleepy little place like Woolpit, then little more than the centre of a farming community that had troubles of its own. Among the biggest of them was wolves. In those days, vicious packs roamed the woods and forests of the British Isles. They were animals that knew little fear. Often they would come close enough to villages to seize livestock.

Farmers resorted to digging wolf traps, then slaughtering the captured beasts and skinning them for their pelts, which were made into warm winter jerkins and tunics. Woolpit was literally ringed with these traps: it was the only hope of stopping the raids. They were checked every day by a team of farm workers.

One morning the team approached a trap that showed signs of something moving inside, but when they got nearer they discovered it wasn't wolves they'd caught. Inside the pit were two young children, a boy and a girl.

It wasn't all that unusual for people to fall into

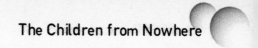

these traps – particularly youngsters who'd disobeyed their parents' warnings about wandering alone in the forest. The pits themselves were well-hidden – they had to be to fool a wary wolf – and if you didn't know their location, it was very easy to put a foot wrong, especially if you were a stranger to the district. The two children were strangers to the district. In fact, they were like no children the farm workers had ever seen.

They were both bright green.

They dressed in green. They had green skin. Their hair was green. They stared up at the adults with fearful green eyes.

The men pulled them out and questioned them, but quickly discovered that while the children could talk, they used some sort of foreign language nobody in the group could understand. Not knowing what else to do, the farmers took the children to the castle of Sir Richard de Calne, the local squire.

By all accounts, Sir Richard was a kindly man. He was astonished by the appearance of the youngsters, but children were children whatever their colour and he decided that like most children they were likely to be hungry. So he ordered his servants to have them fed at once.

It was here that a peculiar similarity with the Kaspar Hauser case began to emerge. Both boy and girl looked ready for a good meal, but stared blankly – and refused to eat – everything that was put in front of them. An increasingly desperate kitchen staff tried dish after dish – root vegetables, beef, pork, even a little of the venison usually reserved for the master. Nothing tempted them.

But then one of the cooks had an inspiration. If the children were green, maybe they were used to green food. He offered them green beans and the two youngsters promptly ate them.

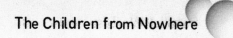

Like Kaspar Hauser who at first refused everything but black bread, this pair survived on a monotonous diet of beans for several days. But, again like Hauser, they were eventually persuaded to eat other foods as well until, after several months, they were eating normally.

All the same, the boy failed to thrive. He didn't seem ill, exactly, but he became increasingly listless, lost weight and eventually died. The girl was an altogether tougher child. She not only survived, but grew and quickly became a popular addition to the squire's household. She proved a bright youngster. One of Sir Richard's staff eventually succeeded in teaching her English. And once she could make herself understood, she told a story every bit as strange as Kaspar Hauser's.

The dead boy, she said, had been her brother. They were born and raised in a Christian land called Saint Martins. Their father was a shepherd and the children often helped him to look after his sheep. One day while they were doing so, a whirlwind sprang up and carried them off, dropping them unharmed near the village of Woolpit.

Apart from the whirlwind, which today sounds like something from the *Wizard of Oz*, the story seemed plausible enough. No-one in Woolpit had heard of a land called Saint Martins, but these were the Dark Ages when few people ever left their villages throughout their entire lifetimes and those who did seldom travelled more than a mile or two. Who was to say Saint Martins didn't exist? It might even have been quite near.

But the girl's description of Saint Martins was as strange in its way as Kaspar Hauser's description of his cramped, dark cell. According to her, it was a country without a sun: there was neither day nor night, just perpetual twilight. And everything in it was as green as she was – trees, plants, grass, animals, houses, even people. Even stranger, Saint Martins was bounded by a river … and beyond it the children could see a land of light.

Even these details were cautiously accepted. The crude maps of the day frequently featured vast areas labelled 'Here Be Dragons', so the fantastic was in many ways a part of everyday life. But then the girl changed her story.

In the second version, the whirlwind vanished,

but, strangely enough, the bizarre description of Saint Martins remained intact. What changed was her account of how she and her brother reached Woolpit.

The story still began with their tending to their father's sheep. While they were out in the fields, they heard distant bells and decided to find out what they were. Together they followed the sound and eventually reached the entrance to an underground passage. The passage both frightened and intrigued them. They hesitated, talked about what to do, then finally went into it.

Darkness quickly closed around them, but they fumbled their way forward until the passage emerged above ground. As the children climbed out, they realised they were in an entirely new world. The familiar gloomy twilight was gone, replaced by brightness and clear skies. There was lots of greenery about, but not *everything* was green. It was the strangest environment they had ever experienced and they set out to explore it with a will. They were still bright-eyed with wonder when they fell into the wolf trap. And there they stayed until the farm hands rescued them.

If the story of the Woolpit children sounds hauntingly familiar, that's because you've heard a version of it before, when you were a child yourself – it gave rise to the old fairy tale of the Babes in the Wood. But there seems little doubt that it actually happened, more or less as I've told it to you now. The discovery of the green boy and girl is recorded, as something of a marvel, by two different medieval historians, Ralph of Coggeshall and William of Newburgh, who reported the intriguing detail that the girl lost her green colouring and grew up to marry a man from Kings Lynn.

But if the story *is* true, what are we to make of it? It seems very likely that the whirlwind of the

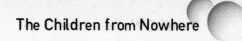

first version was a nonsense, mirroring the children's confusion or possibly just the tendency of youngsters to make up stories. The second version gains some support from the fact that Thetford Forest, Norfolk, which lies to the north-west of Woolpit, is the site of ancient flint mines, which may have been the underground passages the children followed.

It would be reassuring to assume that was all there was to it: a brother and sister stumble on a disused mine shaft and follow it far enough to emerge in an unfamiliar district. But there are very real problems with this down-to-earth explanation. Neither child spoke English at the time of their rescue from the wolf trap and no-one in Woolpit recognised the language they did speak. With their green skin, green hair and foreign language, it's quite clear they did not originate locally – despite the fact that people in the Middle Ages tended to stay close to home, news of a marvel like the birth of green children would have travelled the length of England within a year.

And in particular, what are we to make of their story? While they dropped the detail of the whirlwind, everything else remained absolutely consistent. It may be that they stumbled on an entrance to the flint mines, but if so it's difficult to see how it could have emerged in some other part of Britain.

It's almost as if the green children of Woolpit travelled from another world.

Chapter 3
Things from Nowhere

It isn't just people who seem to appear out of nowhere. On November 10, 1950, a Devon shepherd named Edward Latham was wakened by the barking of his sheepdog. The collie was well trained and never made a fuss unless something was wrong, so Latham got up, got dressed and went outside.

His farm was in the moors, so the environment was fairly bleak. He noted that the sky was clear and, as most nights, there was a chill wind blowing. But despite the dog's unease he could find nothing wrong. He looked around one final time and went back to bed.

When he got up next morning, the dog was

barking again. This time Latham followed the sound to a field about 50 metres from his home. And there the excited collie showed him the body of a sheep. The animal was split across the neck and shoulders as if somebody had struck it with an axe. But it wasn't an axe that killed the sheep. It was a 6-kilogram block of ice that had fallen from the sky at such speed it had buried itself in the ground to a depth of 20-centimetres.

Latham quickly discovered there were many other pieces of ice in the field and along the road beside it, most of them as large as dinner plates.

When Latham reported the loss of his sheep, Britain's Air Ministry stepped in to investigate. In certain weather conditions, ice can form on the wings of aeroplanes and sometimes break off to fall to the ground. But it was soon realised that there were no planes in the area that night, weather conditions had been mild and there was nothing to explain the mysterious appearance of the ice.

Nor was there any explanation when another giant ice cube appeared just two weeks later, this time over London. It crashed through the roof of a Wandsworth garage with such force that the night watchman called the police and reported a bomb explosion. The 'bomb' turned out to be a cubical block of ice, which emerged from a clear sky on a balmy night.

Wherever the ice came from, there's a lot of it up there. In April 1958, a married couple in Napa, California watched with astonishment as huge ice shards from the (clear) sky buried themselves in the earth of their garden. Edwin Groff, a Pennsylvania farmer, watched two 22-kilogram chunks whistle down during his experience of mystery ice. Another mysterious chunk tore a 1-metre hole in the roof of Dominic Bacigalupo's home while he was watching television in

1958, the same year yet another smashed through the roof of a warehouse.

Although meteorologists have no explanation for these ice falls. Peculiar weather conditions can sometimes produce hailstones large enough to smash their way through roofs of houses and even cause serious dents in the metal body work of cars. But that's still a long way from a 22-kilogram block of ice. All the same, most people are inclined to think ice falls must be some sort of freak climatic phenomena But other things appear out of cloudless skies that clearly have nothing to do with the weather.

On a hot summer's afternoon in 1978, for example, Donna Matchett was busy cleaning her swimming pool in Ontario, Canada, when something landed with a thud on the picnic table behind her. She thought it was her dog thumping his tail on the decking, but then there came a cracking sound. Donna turned ... and screamed. There was a molten mass in the middle of the picnic table, with flame shooting from it like a blowtorch. It was very intense, about 46 centimetres long, cylindrical in shape and, incredible for a flame, flat on top. Donna grabbed a garden hose and eventually put it out.

Once she did so, the molten mass shrank to a pitted dark green solid weighing about 113 grams. Analysis showed the substance was polypropylene, a common chemical plastic used in making many household objects. When the incident was publicised, it seemed that three more blobs had mysteriously appeared in the back yards of local people. The largest weighed about 3.6 kg.

The question was where did they come from. Unlike the ice falls, nobody would suggest the possibility of a natural phenomenon, while calls to Toronto International Airport confirmed they could not have come from a passing plane as an aircraft would have needed to be on fire to have dropped something that hot.

Interestingly enough, blobs of stuff, which may or may not be polypropylene, have fallen from the skies for centuries. It usually decomposes very quickly, giving off a particularly bad smell. A few centuries ago in Wales, it was given the name *pewtr ser* or the 'rot of the stars'. Reports going back as far as the 17th century show that it fell, usually in rural areas, in Great Britain, parts of Europe and America, but it may have been appearing for much longer than that. Ancient Egyptian and Greek-Roman texts refer to a substance called 'foam of the moon' (used for magical purposes) which may be the same thing.

But goo and ice does not exhaust the list of things that have fallen mysteriously from the (often totally clear) skies. Here is a little museum cabinet featuring various materials from nowhere:

- **1642** The superstitious citizens of Magdeburg in Germany thought Hell must have opened above them when burning brimstone (sulphur) suddenly rained down on them, setting houses alight and causing widespread panic.

- **1655** Germany again, this time the town of Naumburg where blue silk threads wafted down in a bizarre rain. (The fibres may not actually have been silk, but that's what they looked and felt like, according to the ancient records.)

- **1687** Huge dark flakes, many as big as table tops, floated down along a stretch of the Baltic Sea east coast. This time we know exactly what they were – plates of black algae and infusoria (a class of protozoa – single-celled creatures – found in decaying animal or vegetable matter) somehow bound together to create a nightmare 'snowstorm' that came from … nowhere.

• **1696** It looked like rancid butter. It was greasy, it smelled appalling and it fell, in great quantities, over Ireland.

• **1786** In the Voodoo island of Haiti, black eggs pelted the capital Port-au-Prince in a bizarre hailstorm.

• **1828** Reports from Iran described a rain of animal feed.

• **1846** A drizzle of olive-grey powder covered

Shanghai, China's largest city and some 3,885 *square kilometres* (1,500 square miles) of surrounding countryside. Some experts believe it may have been volcanic in origin. Others don't.

- **1851** It rained beef – yes, beef – on San Francisco.

- **1857** Residents of the town of Ottawa in Illinois dodged on the streets as a rain of cinders fell on them.

- **1940** Residents of Meshchera, in Russia, ran out in delight, heedless of personal injury, when a rain of silver coins began.

- **1957** It was easier for the citizens of Bourges, France: their rain was of genuine 1,000-franc banknotes.

- **1961** Green peaches fell on Shreveport, Louisiana.

- **1968** Pinar del Rio, in Cuba, experienced a mixed rain of mud, wood, glass and pottery.

- **1976** It was banknotes again, this time over Limburg, in Germany.

Believe it or not, this little cabinet of curiosities scarcely begins to scratch the surface of things that have fallen from the sky. Some of them may have a reasonable explanation – that powder over China really could have been volcanic ash and you'd imagine that the banknotes might have blown out of a bank (except that no bank claimed them) – but what about the rest? In medieval France, there was a legend about a country called Magonia, which appeared on no maps because it existed somewhere in the sky.[1] Did the careless residents of Magonia drop beef in 1851? Did an explosion in Magonia shower down wood, glass, pottery and mud in 1968?

It's not so long since scientists insisted *nothing* could fall from the sky, let alone the assortment of junk you've been reading about. As late as the 18th century, a spokesman of the British Academy of Sciences countered reports of a meteorite with the statement: 'Stones cannot fall from the sky because there are no stones in the sky.' Even seeing the meteorite failed to change his mind. He decided the stone had been

---

1 In the 9th Century *Book Against False Opinions Regarding Hail and Thunder*, Archbishop Agobard of Lyons wrote: 'We have seen and heard a lot of people so mad and blind as to believe and to assert that there exists a certain region called Magonia, from which ships, navigating on clouds, set sail to transport back to this same region the fruits of the earth…'

in the ground all along but had been unearthed by lightning (which neatly explained the flash in the sky and the bang when it landed).

But our Magonia moments aren't at all like that. We now know all about meteoric stones from the sky and where they come from. But no-one, repeat *no-one*, has yet put forward a wholly satisfactory explanation for the blobs, beef, ice and assorted items that keep falling on our heads.

And besides, not all of it comes from the sky. Over the past decade, psychical researchers in Britain have become increasingly interested in the phenomenon of Objects Out Of Place, or OOOPs for short. Their investigations started almost as a joke. Most of us are familiar with the experience of leaving something down, then returning to find it's mysteriously disappeared. (The phenomenon is more common as you get older.) You've probably also noticed that sometimes, having searched the house, you return to the place where you thought you'd left it and discover it's come back.

If you're like most people, you've put this down to absentmindedness. Not so, say the

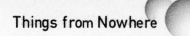

scientists. On all the evidence, it's beginning to look as if small objects really *do* disappear without anyone taking them and really *do* return without anyone putting them back.

The question is: where do they go to, where do they return from?

Chapter 4
Creatures from Nowhere

Whatever the popular song may tell you, it isn't raindrops that keep falling on your head – it's fish. Between 1921 and 1946, the respected ichthyologist (scientific fish expert) Dr E. W. Gudger of the American Museum of Natural History in New York published no fewer than five learned papers in which he studied fish falls from the skies.

Typical of the sort of case he studied was this account from an Indian Army officer named John Harriott, who reported:

In a heavy shower of rain, while our army was on the march a short distance from Pondicherry, a quantity of small fish fell with the rain, to the astonishment of all. Many of them lodged on the men's hats; when General Smith, who commanded, desired them to be collected, and afterwards when we came to our ground, they were dressed, making a small dish that was served up and eaten at the General's table. These were not flying fish, they were dead and falling from the common, well-known effect of gravity; but how they ascended or where they existed, I do not pretend to account. I merely relate the simple fact. [2]

The 'simple fact' of fish falls has been repeated over and over again, world wide. The Reverend Colin Smith of Appin reported on a shower of herring in Argyllshire, Scotland, where the fish were so large and fine that several of the tenant farmers collected them up as presents for their landlord. On another occasion, more than three barrels of herring fry – ranging in length from 4 to 7.5 centimetres – were found scattered over the moss to the north-east of Sheen, Surrey. Like the others, these fish were presumed to have dropped out of the sky, but the Rev. Smith added the interesting observation that none of these

[2] Quoted from *Fortean Studies*, Vol. 2. Steve Moore (ed.) John Brown Publishing, London, 1995.

fish appeared to have been bruised by their fall.

Polynesians on the South Sea island of Tahiti coined the term *topataua* ('rain-drop') to describe a small species of fish collected from waterless hollows in the rocks far from tidal action or river flows. The fish were typically undamaged and sometimes even alive, but the local belief was that they fell from the sky, since there didn't seem to be anywhere else they *could* have come from. In other cases, it was very clear where the fish came from, as in this account:

When I was at work in a field, I perceived the sky darkened with clouds, began to rain a little and a large fish fell from the sky. I was confounded at the sight and soon entered my small cottage... but I came out again as soon as the rain had ceased and found every bit of my hut scattered with fish.

There have been fish falls in Sri Lanka and Singapore. The latter of these two occurred after a violent earthquake and was so plentiful that large numbers of people rushed out to fill their baskets. Investigation afterwards showed fish spread over an area of 20 hectares.

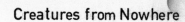

There have been fish falls as far apart as Pomerania (now part of present-day Germany and Poland) and America. One downpour in Louisiana left a line of fish stretching for more than 64 kilometres (40 miles). There is even one report of a frozen fish falling in Germany. Herr Joseph Grimberg of Essen reported, 'During yesterday's hailstorm there fell a hailstone the size of a hen's egg in which an enclosed fish was found frozen.' It turned out to be a species of carp.

Not to be outdone, residents of Hendon, near London, reported a downpour of sand eels.

But widespread though fish falls have been, they're nothing compared with the vast numbers of frogs – yes, frogs – that have appeared out of the blue. On October 24, 1987, for example, Britain awoke to a *Daily Mirror report* on a heavy downpour of pink frogs.

According to the newspaper, residents of Stroud in Gloucestershire stood in amazement while they were pelted with the creatures during what appeared to be a perfectly normal, if a little sudden, cloudburst. The frogs were very much alive. They bounced off umbrellas, hopped across pavements and filled Stroud gardens. Although a little dazed at first, as you might expect, they eventually headed in their hundreds to the nearest rivers.

The Gloucestershire Trust For Nature Conservancy received a report of the extraordinary event from a local resident and sent a naturalist named Ian Darling to investigate. His report showed none of the frogs was more than a few grams in weight and their odd appearance was due to the fact that each and every one of them was an albino (had no colour in their bodies).

We often think of albino animals as white, but the reality is that they are actually colourless – a condition that often shows itself as white. But in the case of the Gloucestershire frogs, their skin was actually transparent – or at least translucent – without a hint of the normal green. The pink colouring was due to the fact that their blood showed through.

Incredibly, they were not the first pink frogs to fall in Gloucestershire. Just two weeks earlier, they fell on Cirencester, which is only a short drive away from Stroud. Although pink frogs are certainly unusual, rains of bog-standard green frogs are now so common that I saw one featured, without explanation or comment, in a Hollywood movie I watched the other night.

Outside of movies, D. F. Garner, of Baltimore, Maryland, USA reported driving through a thunderstorm in Pennsylvania when dozens of tiny frogs pelted his car. Another American, F. J. McManus, reports that when he was a boy on his parents' farm in Minnesota, a storm blew up that looked serious enough for everybody to take cover in the cellar. When the storm passed over, the family came out to find the ground covered in tiny frogs. (There were fish mixed in with that frog fall as well.)

Back in England, Mrs Vida McWilliam of

Parallel Worlds

Bedford witnessed a frog fall near her home during the summer of 1979. The weather was particularly bad, with heavy rain and high winds. While Mrs McWilliam sensibly stayed indoors and consequently didn't see anything unusual actually falling, she discovered next morning that her patio was covered in frogs. There were more frogs in her garden. They were tiny, some green, some black and several of her bushes were covered in frog spawn.

But if Mrs McWilliam only saw the aftermath, there is no doubt at all that frogs come down from the sky. In the summer of 1926, W. A. Walker of Evansville, Indiana, was caught in a sudden thunderstorm while playing golf. Suddenly, along with the rain, he and his companions were pelted with thousands of small, live frogs. Dozens of witnesses watched the frogs that fell on Leicester, Massachusetts, in 1953.

And frogs aren't the only animals to come down out of the sky. Some of their close relatives seem to be living up there as well. In 1683 there were reports of a rain of toads over Norfolk, England. Toads have also fallen in France twice, in 1794 and 1809. Other reptiles to appear mysteriously are lizards, which rained down on Sacramento, California, in 1870 and snakes, which fell on Memphis, Tennessee, in 1877.

Even more mysteriously worms rained down on Randolph County, West Virginia in 1891 while in 1578 yellow mice plunged from the sky at Bergen in Norway. There was a rainfall of lemmings in the same place a year later. Lemmings aren't small. Many of them reach a length of 13 centimetres.

So where do they all come from? Scientists have dreamed up some very ingenious explanations. Two of the most commonly sited are whirlwinds and waterspouts.[3] The idea is that whirlwinds or waterspouts suck up large quantities of fish, frogs or what have you and then deposit them in the form of peculiar rains.

On the face of it, this sounds convincing. There has been at least one instance (in England) where people actually observed fish blown out of a lake during a storm. They didn't fall as rain, but it's not difficult to imagine that they might have, had the storm been a little fiercer. In Norway, there was a reported case of an entire harbour

[3] Waterspouts are spinning columns of water, sometimes hundreds of metres high, drawn up from lakes or seas by high winds.

almost completely emptied of water by a waterspout ... and clearly anything in the water would have gone up with it.

Whirlwinds, which can reach speeds of 480 km/h (300 mph), are known to have carried off the most unlikely things, including cars, sometimes for considerable distances. One flew a 270-kilogram wooden beam a quarter of a mile. A chicken coop ended up over 6 kilometres (4 miles) from its original location while a church spire was swept an almost incredible 27 kilometres (17 miles).

All the same, whirlwind and waterspout theories fall apart when you start to examine them more closely. There are two main problems. The first is the fact that in almost all cases, the creatures that rain down are alive and well. (Remember the report that mentioned the fish weren't even bruised?) People have been killed by whirlwinds while firmly on the ground. It's difficult to see how anything could survive being carried off by one.

But the main problem is that the vast majority of strange rains involve a single creature – fish, frog, mouse or what have you – and sometimes even a single species of a single creature. Fish don't come down accompanied by sand and seaweed as you would expect if they'd been ripped from their natural habitat by a waterspout. Frogs aren't surrounded by grass, twigs, pondweed or anything else you'd expect to find in their normal surroundings.

Many scientists have reacted to this problem by looking for an alternative explanation. Those frog falls in Gloucestershire, for example, happened to coincide (roughly) with more widespread dust falls over England carried by high winds from the Sahara. This led to the theory that the frogs had been carried from the Sahara as well, a habitat not usually noted for its teeming amphibian life. Experts have even thought that the frogs had buried themselves in the sand to escape the heat and then been dyed pink by the red sand crystals – an idea that roundly ignored Mr Darling's discovery that they weren't really pink at all.

Another even dottier notion was that a waterspout had somehow formed over the Sahara – one of the driest spots on earth – and carried the frogs safely all the way to Britain.

Parallel Worlds

None of these ideas – and those mentioned are by no means the silliest to be put forward – come close to answering the basic question. If so many things fall from the sky (and they do) where on earth, or in the sky, do they come from?

Chapter 5
Visitors from Nowhere

On February 8, 1855, a baker in Topsham, Devon, got up early to open his shop. It had snowed in the night and the world was white. These were the days before the invention of the motor car or even the electric light. People tended to rise with the sun and go to bed early. Most nights, there was very little activity, especially in country areas. So footprints in a snowfall first thing in the morning tended to be few and far between. But there were footprints this morning. Or rather there were hoofprints.

The baker noticed them at once. They were small and set about 20 centimetres apart. They followed a dead straight line that headed for his shop. But before the hoofprints actually reached the door of the shop, the trail turned sharply right and ended at a brick wall almost 2 metres high.

The baker began to feel a chill that had nothing to do with the winter temperature. Although it was clearly some cloven-hoofed animal that had made the trail, the prints were too small for a horse or cow. But what made them really creepy was the fact they'd been made by something that walked on two legs, not four. What breed of two-legged creature had cloven hooves?

He walked over to the wall where the trail ended and discovered something more disturbing still. The soft curl of snow on top of the wall bore the imprint of the same tiny hooves … and the trail continued on the far side of the wall.

In fact, the trail stretched all the way across Devon, running north/south for a distance of more than 160 kilometres (100 miles). Nothing stopped the creature. It walked over fields, roads, walls, fences, even houses (the trail continued visibly over the rooftops). The creature, whatever it was, seemed to have begun its walk near Exmouth in the north, and disappeared at Totnes, far to the south, having

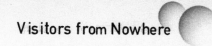

apparently walked all the way across a bay near Powderham Castle in the process.

When the mystery was reported in *The Times*, people's imagination went wild. Letters flooded in suggesting explanations. Somebody thought it might be a kangaroo, escaped perhaps from some zoo. Others voiced the opinion that it might be a fox, or a wolf, or a bird. Nobody bothered to explain how wolves, birds, foxes or even kangaroos would manage to equip themselves with cloven hooves. Or how any animal could manage to travel more than 160 kilometres (100 miles) in a single night. What was it? Where did it come from? And how was it that similar tracks were seen years before in Poland and Scotland?

A large, if superstitious, section of the public came to the conclusion that the Devil had walked across Devonshire. If so, he never came back … at least not to Devonshire. But just over half a century later, something perhaps a little similar turned up in the United States.

At around 2 a.m. on January 17, 1909, insomniac John McOwen of Bristol, Pennsylvania, happened to be looking out of his bedroom window when something very strange attracted his attention. He later described it as, '...a large creature standing on the banks of the canal' and said it looked, 'something like an eagle.' But this description turned out to be misleading. The thing was no eagle and probably not a bird of any sort.

Shortly after the McOwen sighting, a local police officer named James Sackville, spotted the creature. He described it as,'... winged, hopping like a bird, but with strange features and a horrible scream.'

Later that morning, the Pennsylvanian postmaster saw the creature actually flying. It was winging its way across the Delaware River. But what the postmaster described was certainly no bird: 'Its head resembled that of a ram, with curled horns, and its long thick neck was thrust forward in flight. It had long thin wings and short legs, the front legs shorter than the hind.' It had a terrifying call – something between a squawk and a whistle.

What may link the ram-headed, two-legged winged entity with the Devonshire Devil is the fact that a number of Bristol residents later found the creature's *hoof-like footprints* in the snow.

Whatever it was keeps coming back. Little more than a decade after the Pennsylvania sighting, a couple named Mr and Mrs Roger Scarberry were driving at night with friends in West Virginia, when something reflected red in the headlights. As they got closer, they realised to their horror that what had caught their attention was a reflection from the eyes of a hideous, humanoid winged creature. It was over 2-metres tall, grey in colour and equipped with enormous drooping wings and it walked on two legs.

These were among the earliest reports of a creature that has since turned up in many areas of the United States. During the early 1940s, Pennsylvania author Robert Lyman saw one sitting in a road. He later said it looked like a very large vulture, brown, with a short neck and with very narrow wings. After a while it spread wings measuring 6 metres and rose into the air, then flew into the woods.

In 1969, it – or something very like it – was back again. Mrs John Boyle was sitting on her remote cabin porch enjoying the view near Little Pine Creek when a huge, grey-coloured 'bird' landed in the water. She said its wingspan was nearly as wide as the creek ... which would have made it fully 23 metres. After a while the creature rose and flew back into the woods.

Ten years later, the creature was spotted in Texas. The witnesses were two youngsters, 14-year old Jackie Davis and 11-year-old Tracey Lawson. They claimed to have seen a giant 'bird' almost 2 metres high, with shoulders wider than a man's. It was dark coloured, had a bald head with big red eyes and a gorilla-like face.

Needless to say, nobody believed them, but when their parents accompanied them to check out the area next day, they found three-toed tracks nearly 20 centimetres across pressed deeply into the ground.

There is, of course, no species that even remotely fits the description of these weird creatures. But at the same time, the sightings have not come from the depths of the Amazon jungle or the remote regions of Tibet, where it is just possible that an unknown type of animal or bird may live. The 'Mothman', as journalists have now christened the creature, has been seen in some of the most densely populated areas of the United States.

So where do the Mothmen come from?

One chilling possibility is that they may literally come out of nowhere, like the so-called Manila vampire, a case that occurred in 1951 and has remained a mystery to this day.

On May 10 of that year, an 18-year-old girl named Clarita Villaneuva was standing by a street corner in Manila, capital of the Philippines, when she was violently attacked ... by something that wasn't there!

Clarita screamed in shock, then screamed for help. The invisible attacker bit her savagely. In moments she was surrounded by onlookers, most of them drunks and deadbeats, but nobody moved to help her. In fact, it quickly became clear that they thought she was mad. They cheered on her efforts to defend herself and gave each other knowing looks.

Eventually the girl's screams attracted the attention of the police, but they weren't particularly sympathetic either. Clarita was just one of the hundreds of homeless children left stranded on Manila streets at the end of the Second World War, just six years earlier. They grabbed her, hauled her to the nearest station and threw her into a cell.

By this stage Clarita was frantic. She kept screaming at the police that she'd been attacked by a *thing* with bulging eyes and a long, black cape. She wanted them to examine the teeth marks she claimed were visible on her body. The police would have none of it. If the girl wasn't mad, she was clearly on drugs. The only signs on her body would be needle marks. Nobody wanted to waste any time on her.

But there was no calming Clarita down. Now she was shrieking that the thing was coming after her, right through the bars of her locked cell. She was making so much noise now it was quite clear nobody was going to get any sleep that night if something wasn't done. One of the constables unlocked her cell door and led her into the hallway, hoping he might persuade her to stop screaming. And then, as she passed under the overhead light, he saw it.

Incredibly, livid teeth marks began to appear on her upper arms and shoulders. Worse still, each one was surrounded by saliva. The policeman stared for a moment, scarcely able to believe his eyes, then ran to call the Captain. The Captain took one look and promptly sent for the Chief of Police. The Chief of Police had never seen anything like it and dispatched someone to get the Chief Medical Examiner. Meanwhile, whatever it was continued to bite Clarita with savage fury.

The Chief Medical Examiner did not appreciate

being roused from his warm bed in the middle of the night – especially for what sounded like some homeless girl having an epileptic fit. But when he reached the station, he discovered the Mayor of Manila, Arsenio Lacson, was already there and taking the case very seriously indeed.

There was a brief conversation about the possibility that the girl had somehow managed to bite herself while in a fit. That conversation ended when somebody pointed out there were bite marks on her shoulders and the back of her neck, places her own teeth could never reach.

Things settled down eventually, but there was no question of Clarita returning to her cell. She stayed in the front office of the police station under constant observation and sobbed herself to sleep on a bench somewhere in the small hours of the morning.

The following day, the police routine started up again. Whatever might have been happening to the girl, she had still been found wandering the streets and vagrancy was still a criminal offence in Manila. They began to prepare the papers necessary to take her to court. But as this got underway, the girl started screaming again.

Even at this stage there was a lingering suspicion that she might be epileptic. Two burly policemen grabbed her, one on each arm. The Chief Medical Officer, who'd had little sleep the night before, was still there. Both he and the policemen watched with open-mouthed astonishment. No longer could he pretend this was a case of epilepsy: deep bite marks were appearing on the girl's arms, hands and neck – and he could see clearly they were not self-inflicted. The attack lasted fully five minutes, only ending when Clarita fell unconscious to the floor.

The Chief Medical Officer demanded that the Mayor be called back and added that he wanted the Archbishop of Manila there as well. It took the Mayor half an hour to get back, by which time Clarita had regained consciousness. The bites on one hand and both arms had begun to swell. There was severe bruising and continued signs of teeth marks deeply embedded in her flesh.

By now there was no longer any question of court action. The girl obviously needed urgent medical attention. They bundled her into a car and headed for the nearest hospital, some 15 minutes drive away. During the journey, Clarita was attacked again; and this time she claimed her original attacker had been joined by a second bug-eyed creature. Once again everyone else in the car could see the vivid bite marks appearing out of nowhere.

But as Clarita entered the hospital, her nightmare finally ended. The attacks stopped abruptly and she made a slow, but full, recovery from her wounds. She was never attacked again. Whatever had tormented her seemed to have gone back from where they came.

Leaving one vital question still unanswered. Where did her attackers come from in the first place?

Chapter 6
Disappearing Things

If some things seem to turn up out of nowhere, others slip away into nowhere just as mysteriously. The *Iron Mountain* is one obvious example.

The story of the *Iron Mountain*, a Mississippi steamboat, began (and ended) in June 1872. The boat was well named: she was a mountain of a vessel, 59 metres long and 11.5 metres wide. On a bright, calm, summer's morning she finished loading a massive cargo of cotton and molasses at the port of Vicksburg, took on 55 passengers and crew, sounded her whistle then steamed off for Louisville, Cincinnati and Pittsburgh, towing a line of barges behind her.

Parallel Worlds

Workers on the dock watched until she disappeared around a bend in the river, then turned back to other work. The *Iron Mountain* was never seen again.

The first hint that something was wrong was when another paddle steamer, the *Iroquois Chief* almost collided with a string of runaway barges floating downstream. The Captain ordered full emergency power and just managed to get out of the way in time.

While crises like this didn't happen often, they had certainly happened before. Towed barges sometimes broke their rope and were swept away, sometimes before their riverboat crew even noticed. There was a standard procedure adopted by other boats to deal with such a situation. You grabbed the barges if you could, dropped anchor and waited for the parent boat, which was bound to come looking for them eventually. The *Iroquois Chief* chased after the runaways, tied them on, then pulled over to wait.

But the *Iron Mountain* never came. What's more, it quickly became clear that the tow rope *hadn't* broken – it had been cut.

At the time, the Mississippi was probably the

busiest river in America. It was beyond belief that anything sailing its waters could face a mishap without somebody knowing. And in the very unlikely event that an accident did occur without direct witnesses, the evidence would be clear to see. Had the boat's boilers exploded, there would be scattered debris, flotsam and jetsam on the water and the river bank. Had the boat caught fire, the blaze would have been obvious. Had it simply sunk, the 400 bales of cotton loaded on its deck would have covered the river for miles.

Besides, what sort of tragedy would have been so final that not one of its 55 passengers and crew would survive to tell the tale? Yet for all this, it happened. The *Iron Mountain* sailed round a bend in the river and disappeared from the face of the planet. She wasn't the only vessel to do so.

On December 14, 1928, a Danish training ship, the *Kobenhaven* was moored in the harbour of Montevideo, the capital of Uruguay, on the north shore of the Río de la Plata estuary. She was awaiting the arrival of 50 cadets, currently taking part in a ceremony at the city's Danish consulate. Once the cadets appeared, the ship was scheduled to set sail for home where the trainees would become fully fledged seamen.

The boys returned shortly before noon and the ship set sail soon after. She steamed out of the harbour in full view of several small fishing vessels and headed majestically out to sea. But incoming vessels reported no sign of her. There was no wreckage, no distress signals, no lifeboats, no survivors, no time really for a ship that size to sink in what would have been full view of shore.

Like the *Iron Mountain*, the *Kobenhaven* simply sailed off the face of the planet. Where did she go? Perhaps the same place so many ships went when they ventured into the Bermuda Triangle.

The Bermuda Triangle is an area of the North Atlantic Ocean marked by the southern US coast, Bermuda, and the Greater Antilles,[4] which had generated some very disturbing reports over the years.

The trouble seems to have started early, long before the Triangle received its name in 1965. As the *Nina*, the *Pinta* and the *Santa Maria* sailed through the area in 1492, their compasses went haywire and their crews saw weird lights in the

4 The actual area tends to vary depending on the source you consult and is only roughly triangular in shape, but it's a great name, so it has stuck.

sky. But nothing else untoward occurred and the leader of the expedition, Christopher Columbus, urged them on to discover America.

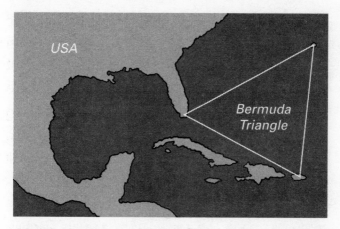

Other vessels weren't so lucky. The first officially recorded loss was the USS *Pickering* which sailed into the Triangle in 1800, but failed to sail out again. Since then, more than 50 ships have disappeared in the area while others have lost their complete crew to float eerily and empty. Where vessels disappeared, no wreckage has ever been found. Where crews disappeared, no explanation has ever been discovered.

But despite what happened to the ships, the Triangle's evil reputation only really peaked in 1945 when the world learned what happened to the five aircraft comprising the US Navy Flight 19.

Flight 19 took off from the Fort Lauderdale Naval Air Station at 2 p.m., December 5 on what was planned as a routine training mission. The weather was good and no one expected any problems. Then, approximately an hour and three quarters later, a senior flight instructor named Lieutenant Robert Cox was preparing to land at Fort Lauderdale when he overheard a radio conversation between two members of Flight 19. One of them asked the other what his compass read. The reply, from airman Captain Powers, was the first sign something might be wrong. Powers said bluntly that he didn't know where they were. He thought the entire flight had got lost after the last turn they made.

At this point, Lieutenant Cox interrupted the radio transmissions to ask what the trouble was. He had an immediate reply from Flight Leader Lieutenant Charles C. Taylor: 'Both my compasses are out. I'm trying to find Fort Lauderdale. I'm over land but it's broken. I'm sure I'm in the Keys, but I don't know how far down.'

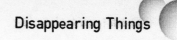

Cox gave him instructions on how to reach Lauderdale and assumed that now Taylor knew where he was, he would be able to get back safely. But Taylor *didn't* know where he was and at 3.45 p.m. he was forced to make a call to the Control Tower at Fort Lauderdale, 'Calling Tower. This is an emergency. We seem to be off course. We cannot see land. Repeat, we cannot see land.'

The Tower Radio Operator asked his position. Taylor responded, 'We are not sure of our position. We cannot be sure just where we are. We seem to be lost.' The radio operator instructed him to assume a bearing due west. Taylor's reply must have sent a chill down his spine, 'We don't know which way is west. Everything is wrong ... strange. We can't be sure of just where we are. We are not sure of any direction. Even the ocean doesn't look as it should.'

At this point, Lieutenant Cox cut in again. He asked Taylor's altitude and volunteered to fly south to meet him. But Taylor suddenly replied that he knew where he was now. 'I'm at 2,300 feet (701 metres),' he said. 'Don't come after me.'

It was the last radio communication and as it was received, a Martin PBM Mariner flying boat neared the Flight's last position. Eyewitness reports from the ship *Gaines Mill* and radar observations aboard the aircraft carrier USS *Solomons* indicate that it exploded in mid air.

A massive, five-day search and rescue mission ensued which employed 252 planes flying 930 sorties and 30 surface craft searching every square metre of sea in which the lost planes could have gone down. There was no sign of any of them. There was no sign of wreckage. There were no survivors. If the Martin Mariner exploded, Flight 19 seems to have disappeared off the face of the earth.

There was a curious sequel to these events on May 8, 1991. Salvage divers found five World War Two aircraft on the ocean floor 16 kilometres (10 miles) off Fort Lauderdale. Four were intact, the fifth broken in half. All sat on the bottom as if they had carefully landed and parked one behind the other. Even the broken one looked as if it had been smashed by subsequent ocean action. Quite clearly, Flight 19 had been found.

Except that it hadn't. On June 4, divers got close enough to photograph the aircraft tail numbers which showed it was not Flight 19 at all but five planes that had disappeared *before* the 1945 incident. Nobody has the least idea what happened to them either.

Although justly famous as an area where mysterious disappearances take place, the record of the Bermuda Triangle pales when compared with that of the so-called Devil's Triangle south of Japan. The area is bounded by a point midway on Japan's eastern coastline, the northern tip of the Philippines to the southwest and Wake Island to the east.

From 1968 to 1972 this deadly Triangle officially claimed a terrifying total of 1,472 small ships (under 2,000 tonnes). Since 1949 the official tally of major ships lost in the area is 40. The number of craft lost in the Devil's Triangle between 1968 and now is more than the total number of ships lost in the Bermuda Triangle since 1800. Between 1949 and 1954, 10 large, fully-crewed ships vanished leaving no trace whatsoever. In 1942 an Imperial Japanese Navy task force consisting of three destroyers and two aircraft carriers mysteriously disappeared.

And planes disappear as well. In March of 1957 the Triangle claimed three within two weeks. Twelve years earlier, a radio transmission from Zero F Wing Commander Shiro Kawamoto leading four planes back to their carrier contained these final, chilling words, 'Something is happening in the sky. The sky is opening up...'

But not just ships and planes. Incredible though it may seem, whole islands have disappeared.

The remote isle of Saxemberg was discovered by Dutch seamen in 1670. It's about 950 kilometres (600 miles) north-west of Tristan da Cunha in the South Atlantic. But while carefully charted by the Dutch, subsequent expeditions failed to find it. Then, more than 130 years later,

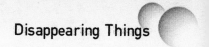

in 1804, it was found again and visited five years later by another ship. Which was the last anyone has ever seen of it.

Isla Grande was discovered in 1675 by Antonio de la Roche 2,413 kilometres (1,500 miles) south east of Buenos Aires. It was visited by the Spaniards who recorded it was inhabited by white, black and brown races. Neither the island nor its inhabitants are there today.

There was an inhabited island called Mayda between Bermuda and the Bahamas in the early 17th century. It's not there now. The Aurora Islands are located at (North Island) 52.378S:47.43W; (Central Island) 53.2S:47.55W; (South Island) 53.2S: 47.57W. They were discovered in 1762, seen again in 1790, visited and charted in 1794, seen again in 1856 and 1892. But you can check those coordinates on a modern map and you won't find them today.

St Brendan's Isle, off the west coast of Ireland, is usually described as a myth. It certainly doesn't exist today. But the American professor Clarence Quinn-Berger found British admiralty records showing it had been visited in the 18th century.

Chapter 7
Disappearing People

There are, of course, always those who insist that ships, planes and islands don't disappear into thin air, so there must be some other explanation … even though they can't quite think of it at the moment. But for many of the people who disappear from the face of the Earth every year, no other explanation is forthcoming. A typical case history concerns the British knight, Sir Benjamin Bathurst.

Sir Benjamin was a British diplomat and ambassador to the court of the Austro-Hungarian Empire whose career ended abruptly in 1809 under circumstances that were positively bizarre.

Early in that year, he had been dispatched to

Vienna to help negotiate an alliance between Britain and Austria, aimed at calling a halt to Napoleon who seemed at the time on the point of conquering Spain. By November he was recalled to London to report progress.

In those days the journey was made by carriage and boat and took several days. One of the stops was the German town of Perleberg, where Sir Benjamin and his party stayed at the local inn. The following day as arrangements were made to depart, his coachman brought the coach to the front of the inn where his valets and secretary took their places by the door of the coach. Sir Benjamin appeared at the inn door and came down the steps to inspect the horses. Having examined the animals on the near side of the coach, Sir Benjamin walked around the heads of the horses to examine the remaining two ... and vanished from the face of the Earth.

There was no sound, no cry for help, no body to bear witness to a murder. Guards posted at both ends of the narrow street confirmed that Sir Benjamin had not passed them, nor had anybody else. But most mysterious of all was that the secretary and valets all stated categorically that their master had simply disappeared. (A notice subsequently appeared in a Hamburg newspaper claiming Sir Benjamin had written a letter to his friends stating he was alive and well, but this turned out to be untrue. No-one was able to trace the source of the notice, although Napoleon himself went on record as denying that Bathurst had been abducted by French agents.)

Sir Benjamin was by no means the first recorded disappearance, or even the most mysterious. About 40 years earlier a man named Owen Parfitt suffered a massive stroke that left him almost completely paralysed and wholly unable to walk. Since his condition was well beyond the medical techniques of the day, the most he could look forward to on warm summer evenings was to sit outside his sister's home and admire the view. Typically he wore just his nightshirt and sat on a folded greatcoat. And one evening he disappeared.

His sister Susannah heard a storm approaching and went out with a neighbour to bring Owen in. But he wasn't where she'd left him, although the folded greatcoat was still on his chair. Farm workers who had been hay making across the road could throw no light on the disappearance; Owen was incapable of moving on his own and there was no trace of him from that day on.

No one actually witnessed the disappearances of Parfitt or Bathurst. In 1815, inmates of the Weichselmunde Jail, in Prussia, watched enviously as one of their colleagues escaped as if he'd been beamed out by Captain Kirk of Star Trek. The prisoner was a valet named Diderici, jailed for impersonating his master.

Diderici was one of the prisoners who were allowed exercise privileges in the prison yard, but only so long as he remained shackled. One day he was walking in a line around the yard, his legs in chains, when he suddenly began to fade. Within seconds he was invisible. His chains fell to the ground with a clang. Nothing was ever seen of him again.

As a prominent man, Sir Benjamin Bathurst's disappearance caused a sensation. The way Diderici faded away brought him a degree of fame in his own day. Others have vanished with far less fuss.

In the early evening of December 12, 1829, a former Chief Justice of the US Supreme Court,

Parallel Worlds

75-year-old John Lansing, left his New York home to post some letters. He was never seen again. A massive search was made but he was never found.

There is, of course, the possibility that Judge Lansing was abducted or murdered (even though the authorities never unearthed the slightest clue to his disappearance) but there have been a number of cases in which this sort of explanation just won't do. One was the case of Orion Williamson a farmer In Selma, Alabama, USA. In July 1854, Orion got out of his chair on the front porch of his farmhouse, and set out over a field to bring his horses in from the pasture. His wife and child watched him walk across the field, two neighbours on the other side of the field waved at him, and right before their very eyes, Williamson disappeared without a trace. A massive search was made using bloodhounds, but no trace of Williamson was ever found.

Something similar seems to have happened to James Worson, a shoemaker from Leamington Spa in the Midlands. In 1873, he bet some friends that he could run the 25.5 kilometres (16 miles) from his hometown to Coventry and back again.

Worson set out with three of his friends following in a cart. A few miles down the road, he suddenly stumbled, began to pitch forward ... and disappeared. His friends searched frantically, but no trace was ever found.

In the same year, one couple came close to vanishing in circumstances that may throw some light on the other cases.

During December, 1873, Mr and Mrs Thomas B. Cumpston, an elderly couple from Leeds, were arrested for disorderly behaviour in the early hours of the morning at the railroad station in Bristol. The charge is a little misleading. This was the Victorian era and the fact that the couple were outside in their nightgowns was enough to get them arrested. They were both bewildered and frightened.

Parallel Worlds

At the police station, they made a statement to the effect that they had checked in at the Victoria Hotel the previous day. In their room they were disturbed by a curious deep, booming sound. They complained to the management who also heard the sound but could offer no explanation and lost interest when it stopped. The Cumpstons lost interest as well and went to bed.

But at 3 a.m. they were wakened by the noise again. Alarmed now, they jumped out of bed. Immediately the sound grew louder. They called loudly for help, but their shouts seemed strangely muffled. All at once, the floor began to open and Mr Crumpston felt himself being pulled into it. His wife grabbed him in the nick of time and they both fled in panic through a window. Once outside, they ran into the nearby railroad station ... where they were subsequently arrested.

Whatever it was that tried to suck the Crumpstons in – or something very like it – seems to have appeared again and again throughout human history. Towards the end of November in 1886, for example, four farmers – a father and his three sons – were hard at work pulling corn in their fields near Edina, Missouri, USA, when lightning flashed out of the cloudless sky. In an instant, one of the sons was dead, another seriously injured and the father hurt.

Weather experts will tell you lightning *can't* flash from a cloudless sky: it requires the electrical potential of a thunderhead to form. But the mystery of what it was that *looked* like a lightning flash, pales to insignificance before the mystery of what happened to the third son. He disappeared without a trace. There was no body, not even a pile of ash to suggest he'd been killed. One moment he was simply there, the next he was gone.

The other family members were too shocked, too injured or too dead to be of very much help as eyewitnesses, but similar incidents have happened again, sometimes with witnesses, sometimes without.

It was springtime in Paris, 1889, when a distraught Englishwoman entered the British Embassy to report her mother missing. She and her mother had been passing through Paris on their way back from India, and had checked into a hotel where her mother had been taken ill.

Parallel Worlds

The hotel doctor examined her then sent the daughter to fetch some medicine. But eerily, when she returned the hotel staff denied ever having seen her mother. A helpful clerk showed her that only her own name was in the register.

Half crazy with worry, the girl insisted on seeing her mother's room. But she found it was not the one she remembered. She then demanded to see the hotel doctor, but he denied ever having met her before. Unable to make her story believed, the young woman was sent to an asylum in England.

An even more mysterious case occurred in France the following year. Louis Le Prince, a pioneer of motion picture technology stepped on a train and never got off again. Seven years after his disappearance he was finally declared dead.

And still the reports keep rolling in. On May 7, 1893, Miss M. Scott was walking to meet her sister near St Boswells, in Roxburghshire, when she noticed a tall man in a black suit walking ahead of her. She watched him turn a corner, but since the hedge was low the top half of his body remained visible. At least it remained visible for a moment, then the man abruptly disappeared while Miss Scott was still watching him.

Miss Scott thought he had tripped and fallen and ran to see if she could help. The man in the black suit wasn't there, but running in the other direction was Miss Scott's sister who exclaimed excitedly that she had just seen a man disappear.

It happened again in 1895, this time to an Oxford man named John Osborne. On the last day of March, he was walking on the road to Wolverton when he heard hoof beats behind him. He turned to see who was coming and realized to his dismay that a rider was having real difficulty controlling his horse. Osborne dived for cover – a runaway horse could kill you – but he needn't have worried. Before he took three steps, both horse and rider disappeared into thin air.

Five years later, a man named Sherman Church disappeared into thin air while at work. According to the *Chicago Tribune*, Mr Church was an employee of the Augusta Mills in Battle Creek, Michigan, USA. For most of the day – January 5, 1900 – he was at his desk, working on some papers. When he finished, he got up and walked from his office into the main mill. At which point he vanished. Searchers virtually tore the mill apart in their efforts to find him, but there was no clue to what happened or where he went.

It may be that somebody – or *something* – is involved in these disappearances. On Christmas Eve, 1909, an 11-year-old boy named Oliver Thomas went into the yard of his home at Rhayader, Wales, to fetch some water from the well. Suddenly his parents heard him scream, 'Help, help, they've got me!' But who got Oliver was never discovered. His footprints halted abruptly half way to the well, as if he had vanished into thin air.

Getting water from a well seems to be a particularly dangerous occupation. Another 11-year-old named Oliver – Oliver Larch this time – left his house in South Bend, Indiana, USA to fetch water. His parents heard a scream, rushed out at once … and discovered he had disappeared. The same thing happened in Quincy, Illinois, during November 1878. A 16-year-old boy named Charles Ashmore went out to get some water from the family well and didn't come back. His father and his sister went to look for him, but all they found were footprints

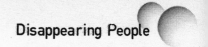

in the snow, leading halfway to the well, where they abruptly stopped. Charles was never seen again.

More and more reports kept coming in from all countries of the world. A particularly intriguing case happened in Canada and the victim (if that is the right word) was the prosperous owner of the Toronto Grand Opera House, Ambrose Small. He arrived for work, walked into his office and closed the door behind him. He never came out again. The first caller of the day discovered the office was now empty. Although there were employees constantly in the outer office, no one saw their boss leave, no-one saw him in the street... in fact no one ever saw him again.

Curious disappearances continue to occur right up to our own day. In December 1, 1946, 18-year-old Paula Welden was walking near Glastonbury, Somerset, when she was spotted by a middle-aged couple about 100 metres behind her. They lost sight of her briefly when she disappeared behind a rocky outcrop, but when they reached the site a few moments later, there was no sign of the young student at all. She was never found.

Parallel Worlds

During the winter of 1949, an old US soldier named Tetford was travelling back by bus from St Albans in Vermont to his home at Bennington, when he dozed off in his seat. Fourteen other passengers on the crowded bus said they saw him there, but when the vehicle reached its destination, his luggage was on the rack, a timetable lay open on his seat, but Mr Tetford himself had disappeared.

Disappearing from a crowded bus is bad enough, but in 1975, a woman named Martha Wright managed to disappear from a car. Her husband, Jackson, was driving from New Jersey to New York through the Lincoln Tunnel. He pulled over to wipe the windscreen and Martha said she'd wipe the back window. She climbed into the back seat and when Wright glanced round, she was gone.

Another example was the case of Graham Marden, a successful Dorset businessman. On a cold January day in 1989, he was driving on the M27 near Southampton when he noticed he was running low on fuel. He pulled into Rownham's service station, filled the tank of his new Volkswagen Polo and used his credit card to pay

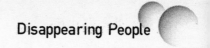

the bill. As he was leaving, he stopped and asked if he could use the Men's Room.

The attendant gave him directions, Mr Marden found the Men's Room and went in. After a while, the cashier noticed the red Volkswagen was still blocking the pumps and went to the Men's Room to see if his customer was all right. There was no answer when he knocked on the door and when he tried it, he found it was locked on the inside. He knocked again, still without an answer, then, with growing concern, went to get his passkey.

He unlocked the door to find the Men's Room completely empty. Bewildered as well as concerned, he phoned the police and told them his strange tale. They arrived soon after with tracker dogs and searched the entire district. There was no sign of Mr Marden (who never turned up again) and no clue as to how he might have disappeared from inside a locked room.

Chapter 8

Mass Disappearances

On January 28, 1914, James Regan, a passenger on board the liner *Prinz Heinrich* mysteriously disappeared in mid-voyage on his way from Marseilles to Naples. Strangely he took his suitcases with him, and no one on board the packed ship saw him fall overboard. The case is a strange one, but disappearances aboard ship involving all passengers and crew are almost commonplace. The most famous example is the *Mary Celeste*.

On November 5, 1872, 37-year-old Captain Benjamin Spooner Briggs sailed the half-brig out of the harbour with a crew of eight, his wife and

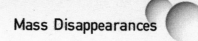

2-year-old daughter all on board. The weather was bad and they were forced to anchor for a time a short distance from port, but on November 7, they got underway again. The ship was bound for Genoa, Italy, with a cargo of 1,700 barrels of alcohol.

Briggs was an experienced seaman – the *Mary Celeste* was his third command – but on February 15, 1872, the ship was discovered drifting by the crew of the *Dei Gratia*. She was slightly damaged – hatch covers had disappeared and there was water between decks – but not nearly enough to explain what had happened.

Although some of the ship's records were missing, a chart was discovered in the First Mate's cabin accompanied by a slate log which showed the *Mary Celeste* had passed the island of Santa Maria (in the Azores) around 8 a.m. on the morning of November 25. For more than three and a half months, the little brig appeared to have been drifting and was now almost 965 kilometres (600 miles) from her last marked position.

Rumours persist that the crew of the *Dei Gratia* found half-eaten meals on the tables and a cat asleep on one of the bunks, but this is now impossible to prove. What is true is that the Captain's bed was unmade, as if he had left in a hurry, and the cargo of alcohol was intact. Rather more mysteriously, there were strange marks on the bow of the ship just above the water line.

None of her crew or passengers was ever found.

The *Mary Celeste* was not the only ship to have lost her passengers and crew in strange circumstances, just the most famous. On August 17, 1840, for example, the merchant ship *Rossini* was found drifting in the Bahamas. She was carrying a cargo of wines, fruits and silks – all in perfect condition. Ship's log was intact, but gave

no hint of what might have happened and a cat, several chickens and two canaries were still alive on board, if somewhat hungry. Nothing has since explained what happened to the ship's crew.

Nothing has explained what happened to the Dutch schooner *Hermania* either. The ship was found drifting off the coast of Cornwall in 1849, minus her masts and crew. Any theory that they might have abandoned ship was disproved by the fact that the lifeboat was still on board.

Just six years later, on February 28, 1855, the *James B. Chester* was found abandoned in mid-Atlantic. All the lifeboats were still on board with not the slightest indication that anybody had ever

tried to use them, but when the ship was searched, its compass and all its papers were missing. There were also clear signs that members of the crew had cleared their personal possessions from drawers and cupboards as if they were planning to go on a journey. The ship herself was undamaged: indeed, she was reported to be 'in fine condition'.

The Atlantic is a big place where anything might happen, but the English Channel is so narrow you can swim across it (assuming you're fit, well-greased and accompanied by a boat in case something goes wrong). All the same, in October 1917, the *Zebrina* managed to lose her entire crew on the brief crossing despite the fact that the weather was fine and everything seemed in good order.

The supply ship *Hesperus* managed to hold onto its crew, but sailed into a mystery over Christmas, 1900, when she dropped anchor off the Isle of Mor, in Scotland, and sent lighthouse keeper Joseph Moore to find out why the light hadn't worked for the past eleven days.

Three keepers manned the lighthouse on Mor, but when Moore arrived, all three had

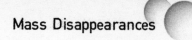

disappeared. Apart from the fact that the light was switched off, everything seemed to be in perfect working order. Weather gear was missing, suggesting the men had gone outside for some reason, but there was no sign of them on the little island.

You don't have to be near the sea for a large group of people to disappear. In March, 1848, an explorer named Ludwig Leichhardt led an expedition of several men and more than 70 pack animals into Australia's Central Desert and, despite all precautions and considerable experience, never led them out again. Aboriginal rock paintings suggest the expedition made good progress for some hundreds of miles, but after that it simply disappeared.

The Central Desert is a huge wasteland capable of swallowing up the unwary (although such a large expedition would be expected to leave some trace), but the mystery didn't stop there. A professional ranger named Zac Mathias organised an expedition of his own in 1975 in an attempt to find the original rock paintings and hence some clues to the missing men. Just before it was due to set out, Mathias himself vanished without trace.

However strange the circumstances, there's always the temptation to think of people who disappear in a wilderness, desert or ocean, as being the victims of natural causes. But what are we to make of the people who have disappeared as far from the wilderness as you are as you read these words?

Such disappearances have been going on for a very long time. One of the earliest on record concerns the 'Unlucky Ninth' – the Roman Army's IX Hispania Legion. In AD 117, it was part of the occupying forces Rome had sent to Britain. It consisted of tough, battle-hardened veterans and was a natural choice to send north to fight the Picts, savage tribesmen who had been causing so much trouble that the Emperor decided they needed to be taught a lesson.

A total of 4,000 men marched through the Scottish village of Dunblane en route to the confrontation ... and disappeared without a trace.

Afterwards, the Picts claimed no victory. Indeed, they claimed no battle had ever taken place. There were no bodies, no pieces of equipment, no dispatches and relief columns sent to find them questioned the natives in vain. It is incredible that 4,000 men could simply melt into nothingness, but that seems to be exactly what happened. Not one soldier from the Unlucky Ninth was ever seen again.

It seems the Romans set a trend for disappearing soldiers which has continued up to modern times. During the War of the Spanish Succession (1701–1714) 4,000 troops managed to disappear in the Pyrenees. No bodies were ever found, not a scrap of equipment was ever seen again.

In 1858, 600 French troops were marching towards Saigon, Vietnam, when, some 24 kilometres (15 miles) from the city, they simply disappeared. Once again no bodies or equipment were ever found.

In 1915, during the Battle of Gallipoli, three members of the New Zealand Field Company watched a battalion of the Royal Norfolk Regiment march up the hillside at Suvla Bay in Turkey. There was low-lying cloud on the hill – one of the witnesses described it as being shaped a little like a loaf of bread. The British soldiers marched into the cloud … and never marched out again. As the last man disappeared, the witnesses saw the cloud slowly rise into the sky. No one remained below, nor was there any sign of the battalion's supplies and equipment.

When the First World War ended, the British Government demanded the return of their troops from Turkey, but the Turks simply replied that they had not captured the men from the Royal Norfolk, nor, indeed, knew anything at all about them. Interestingly, of the 34,000 men killed at Gallipoli, only 6,000 graves are known. The remaining 28,000 are still missing.

In 1939, after Japan invaded China, a group of 3,000 Chinese troops vanished two hours south of Nanking. They were in radio contact with base at the time, but nothing in their messages suggested anything was wrong. Subsequent investigation found the men's weapons, equipment and cooking fires, but no sign of the troops themselves. Japanese sources later confirmed there had been no fighting or enemy contact in the area.

But you and your friends don't have to be in anything as dangerous as an army to vanish from

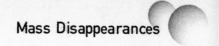

the face of the Earth. Almost any group of people can disappear without explanation.

In North Carolina, for example, a colony founded by 100 English settlers in 1587 somehow disappeared. John White, the colony's governor, sailed back to England for supplies. There was a war between England and Spain at the time, which meant he didn't get back to America until 1591 ... and discovered that the colony no longer existed. But as in similar cases, there was no indication of violence or any other reason for their disappearance.

The disappearance of 100 people is bad enough, but even more mysterious is the disappearance of a thriving fishing village of 2,000 inhabitants. The mystery was discovered in November, 1930, when a trapper named Joe Labelle paid a call on an Eskimo village he knew on the shores of Lake Anjikuni in northern Canada. But when he arrived, the village was deserted.

The villagers had not left long, since one fire was still smouldering. Yet there were no footprints in the snow, no provisions had been taken, and the village's sled dogs had all starved to death. More peculiar still, the graves of the Eskimos' ancestors had been emptied.

One group disappearance was actually witnessed. It happened at Stonehenge in August, 1971, when a group of hippies pitched tents inside the circle and settled down to stay the night. At around 2 a.m., a violent thunderstorm began. Two witnesses, a policeman and a farmer, reported that a lightning bolt struck the stones, which lit up briefly with a strange blue light. There were screams from the campers and both witnesses rushed to the scene. There they found the remains of the tents and a sodden campfire, but every hippy had disappeared.

So ... people, animals, machines, natural objects have all appeared out of nowhere or vanished into nowhere, often in alarming numbers. The questions we have asked over and over in this book are *Where do they come from? Where do they go to?*

One man, a world-famous scientist, may already have supplied us with the answer.

Chapter 9
Einstein's Revolution

In 1895, a 16-year-old German boy wrote an essay that was destined to change the world. The boy's name was Albert Einstein.

Four years earlier, at the tender age of 12, young Einstein had vowed to devote his life to solving the riddle of the universe, but didn't really seem to be following up very well. By the time he reached 15, his grades in history, geography and languages were so poor that he'd been forced to leave school without a diploma.

All the same, two of his uncles managed to stimulate his interest in mathematics and science, so that he resumed his education in Switzerland at the Federal Polytechnic Academy of Zurich. It was there he wrote his essay, the content of which was so remarkable – and so obscure – that it went wholly unappreciated not only by his teachers and family, but also to some extent by young Einstein himself. With no encouragement from anybody, he set the essay aside and forgot about it ... at least for the time being.

By the spring of 1900 (now aged 21) he had graduated and become a Swiss citizen. He took a job as a maths teacher, but it lasted only two months – to his dying day, Einstein maintained that while he was interested in mathematics, he wasn't very good at it.

He cast around a bit and eventually found himself low-paid office work. It wasn't much of a job, but it left him with lots of time on his hands. One of the things he did with it was to expand his half forgotten essay into the Special Theory of Relativity. This was in 1905. By 1916, he has published his second (General) Theory of Relativity and revolutionised scientific thought forever.

If you don't understand Einstein's Theories of Relativity, you're in good company. In his own day, most scientists didn't understand them either; and even today, a century or more after the first was published, they remain far beyond the reach of the general public. But that doesn't matter. What matters is that Einstein's General Theory of Relativity predicted the existence of Black Holes.

Nobody knew about Black Holes in those days, nobody dreamed they might even be possible. But the General Theory of Relativity put forward a whole new way of looking at the universe. Instead of thinking of time and space as separate, Einstein linked them together so they became parts of the same thing. He called this thing the spacetime continuum and showed (mathematically) that it was distorted by matter.

What this means is that wherever you have a lump of matter – like a planet or a star – the spacetime continuum around it bends a little, an effect you and I experience as gravity. The gravity that keeps you from floating off the Earth[5] isn't a force: it's the distortion of

[5] With this book in your hot little hands.

spacetime caused by the mass of our planet.

Which is all very fine for a little planet like ours, or even a little star like our Sun, but if you put enough matter together in one place, the spacetime continuum doesn't just bend, it actually rips apart. The tear that's left becomes what we now call a Black Hole.

For a long time after Relativity was accepted as a fact of scientific life, nobody knew whether Black Holes existed in our universe or were just one of those mathematical peculiarities that sometimes arise in physics showing something that *might* be possible, but isn't really. The term 'Black Hole' wasn't even in use until 1967. But

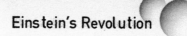

gradually, astronomers came to see how the maths might relate to the cosmos they were currently exploring.

The secret turned out to be that a really large star – something several times bigger than our own Sun – eventually falls prey to its own gravity. Like somebody who gets so fat he can't stand up any more, a massive star will begin to collapse under its own weight. At a certain size, it collapses into a neutron star – essentially one huge atomic nucleus with all the sub-atomic particles squeezed together to make the heaviest material in the known universe.

You'd imagine nothing could beat that, but if you start with a really massive body, the collapse doesn't end with a neutron star: it continues to get smaller and smaller in measured size, but more and more massive in weight, until it disappears altogether, ripping the fabric of spacetime and generating so much gravity that not even light (the fastest thing in the universe) can generate a high enough escape velocity to get away. What's left isn't so much a collapsed star as the *absence* of a collapsed star. What's left is a Black Hole.

At least that was the theory. But figuring out how a Black Hole *might* form was a long way from proving that one actually *had* formed somewhere in the universe. As you might imagine, Black Holes are very difficult to detect. You can't see them with an optical telescope, for one thing, since they don't give out any light. But they *do* give out other radiation, including X-rays, and their massive gravitational field can often cause nearby objects to behave in peculiar ways.

In 1971, astronomers noticed peculiarities in the orbit of the blue supergiant Cygnus X which led them to conclude it had an invisible companion. They discovered the dark star was generating massive amounts of X-rays and had a gravitational pull far beyond its apparent size. The penny suddenly dropped: they had found their first Black Hole. Since then, many more have been discovered.

You may think all this is light years away from the mysteries of vanishing people, but bear with me. Once Black Holes were shown to be a physical reality (as opposed to just a theory) scientists began to study them with enormous enthusiasm. Although no one has yet made a close approach to a Black Hole – and perhaps never will – hard work and mathematics show that in its vicinity many laws of physics, and just about all the laws of common sense, break down completely.

One solution to the equations suggested that anything caught by the massive gravity of a Black Hole wouldn't simply be crushed, but sucked through the very fabric of spacetime to emerge in a wholly different universe. For such a theory you need to assume another, second universe somehow parallel to this one with, somewhere in its heart, a White Hole spewing out matter as it matches the Black Hole sucking matter in.

This was not an idea that appealed to many scientists, including Einstein himself who considered the possibility that there were things wrong with his basic theory. But when he could find nothing wrong, he was intellectually honest enough to publish a paper that placed the whole of his enormous reputation behind the idea of a parallel universe.

But the matter didn't end there. Einstein's calculations were based on a static Black Hole. Which is fine for physicists, but simply won't do for astronomers who have long noted that very few bodies in the universe are actually static. Almost all of them spin and that includes neutron stars. Any star that collapsed beyond the neutron stage would carry with it its spin. And that meant Black Holes in the real universe must be spinning too.

Armed with this knowledge, an Australian physicist named Roy P. Kerr did the maths on spinning Black Holes and discovered that each and every one of them must be the focal point not just of a single parallel universe, as Einstein had concluded, but of an *infinite number* of parallel universes. He also discovered that all but one of them could, in theory, be reached from this one.

The idea that there might be parallel universes (with parallel worlds inside them) was so bizarre most scientists quietly ignored it. Mathematical calculations were all very well, but in this instance they didn't seem to have much application to the real world of telephones, office blocks and double-decker buses.

But then something happened that brought parallel worlds just a little bit closer to home.

Chapter 10
The Impossible Experiment

Relativity Theory is the branch of modern physics that deals with large things – the birth and death of stars, the orbits of cosmic bodies, astronomical distances and so on. The branch that deals with small things – electrons, bosons, quarks and mesons, the whole world of particles smaller than a single atom – is Quantum Mechanics.

Several years after the mathematical basics of Quantum Mechanics were established, Quantum physicists carried out an experiment that produced results so weird they baffled a whole generation of scientists. The experiment, as clearly described and simplified as I can manage, was this. Imagine, on one side of the room, a particle generator. You don't really have to know what this looks like, but for the sake of the picture in your head, think of it as a gun that will shoot out a stream of sub-atomic particles.

On the other side of the room imagine a target. This target is specially wired so that when a sub-atomic particle strikes it, a counter trips. This means you can measure how many of the particles fired by the gun actually reach the target.

Now imagine that you set up a screen between the gun and the target. The screen is manufactured from a material that blocks particles completely, so you make a couple of slits in it to allow some through. You also set it up so you can open and close each slit separately. You have now more or less set up the experiment that produced impossible results. Here's what happened:

At the time the experiment was carried out, sub-atomic particles were thought of as very tiny cannon balls. If you fire a stream of tiny cannon balls at a screen with slits in it, common sense will tell you that if both slits are open, twice as

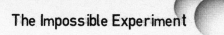

many cannon balls are likely to get through than if you only open one.

But when the experiment was actually carried out, it showed that more cannon balls got through if only *one* slit was open. Since that was quite impossible, they tried the experiment again … and the same thing happened. It continued to happen, right on cue, every time the experiment was repeated.

To make sense of this, the scientists started to wonder if they might be wrong about the nature of sub-atomic particles. You have to appreciate nobody had ever seen one. Maybe, they thought, particles weren't little cannon balls at all, but something else entirely.

One possibility was wave forms. A wave form is exactly what it sounds like: the sort of thing you've watched breaking on the seashore every time you go on holiday. A little cannon ball could only go through one slit at a time, but a wave (which is stretched out) could go through both. This meant that you would get no more hits on the target when two slits were open than you would when you only opened one. Each wave shot from the gun would split apart to get through both slits, then get back together again on the other side.

And actually, when you start to think about it, some of these split waves would collide with each other. When you get a collision between waves, they cancel each other out. So *fewer* waves would get through two slits than one ... exactly what the experiment showed.

That seemed to solve the mystery, except for one thing. The particles, which behaved like waves while they were passing through the two slits, promptly turned back into little cannon balls immediately afterwards. A wave striking the target would hit it all at once, exactly like those waves breaking on a beach.

But the experiment showed this didn't happen. You could see where the particles hit the target and they hit it like little cannon balls.

Physicists lived for years with the uneasy knowledge that particles behaved like particles in certain circumstances and like waves in others. They *knew* this happened, because their experiments told them so, but it just didn't make much sense.

It made so little sense, in fact, that they began

to wonder if the 'wave' existed in the real world at all. Was it possible it might just be a mental convenience that helped them keep track of what they were seeing? Even though it looked like a wave and walked like a wave and quacked like a wave, it might actually be an example of the way the human mind puts things in proper order.

To understand this theory, you need only look out through the window. You see trees, grass, fields, a stream and so on. But in fact you're not seeing any of those things. What's happening is that light bounces off a whole series of different structures out there. Having bounced, it hits your eye, which triggers an electrical pulse along a nerve track feeding information into your brain. Your brain is peppered with information every second of your day – raw information, coming in from all over the place: sights, sounds, smells, sensations. It's a big mess, but what your brain does is to organise things so they make sense. It does that by imposing *patterns* on the information.

Maybe, the physicists thought, the so-called 'particle wave' was just one of those patterns, maybe it was really a bunch of possibilities that behaved in a wave-like manner. In other words, the basic particle was still a little cannon ball, but instead of simply watching what it did, scientists were looking at all the things that could happen to a little cannon ball, and their minds were organising them to look like a wave. They started to talk about Quantum particles as if they were *probability* waves.

Physicists are often intelligent and subtle people and this sort of thinking isn't all that easy to follow. But if you apply it to the troublesome double-slit experiment, you can see the attraction. Once you buy the idea of probability waves, you can go back to thinking of particles as little cannon balls.

As each little cannon ball approaches the two open slits in the screen, the probability wave (which really only exists in the mind of the observer) represents the different possibilities open to the particle – whether it passes through the top slit or the bottom, whether it strikes the screen and is absorbed or whether it just bounces off. The probability wave doesn't tell you where the particle will go, only where it's

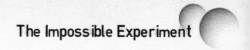

most *likely* to go.

I don't know how clear I've managed to make all that, but if you didn't follow it, it doesn't matter. What matters is the theory of probability waves explained what happened in the impossible experiment. (Probabilities were bound to change from a situation where one slit was opened, to a situation where you opened two.) The only problem left was how probability waves – which only exist in your mind, remember – managed to cancel each other out like physical waves.

In 1957, a young American physicist named Hugh Everett came up with the answer. In a blindingly simple argument, he said that if two probabilities could interfere with one another, that meant they had to have an actual existence in the real world, whatever everybody believed. But since there's no way two probabilities that contradict each other can exist in our universe, it follows logically that there must be a second, parallel universe to house the second probability.

Everett's colleagues were slow to take the idea on board, but today, half a century on, it's probably true to say that a majority of scientists believe parallel universes, parallel worlds, are very likely, even if currently unproven.

Probably because of Einstein's Black Hole discoveries, many people tend to think of parallel worlds as somehow 'out there'. Our nearest Black Hole is, thankfully, many light years away, so any parallel world must be light years away as well.

But the point about a parallel world is that it really *is* parallel. It runs alongside this universe, which means it's closer to you now than the tip of your nose.

And there is some (controversial) evidence that a secret department of the US Military once tried to take advantage of that fact.

Chapter 11
The Philadelphia Experiment

One of the most bizarre yet persistent rumours about the activities of the American Military is the story of the USS *Eldridge*. Officially commissioned on August 27, 1943 as DE-173 (the 'DE' stands for Destroyer Escort), the vessel was of a class designed to protect convoys from submarines. If the incredible story is true, the USS *Eldridge* may have entered into and returned from a parallel world.

The account first surfaced as a result of Dr. Morris K. Jessup's 1955 book, *A Case for UFOs*. A reader who called himself Carlos Miquel Allende (his real name was Carl Allen) claimed in a letter to Jessup to have witnessed a secret US

Navy experiment involving Einstein's Unified Field Theory. (Throughout his life, Einstein was haunted by the belief that there had to be a connection between gravity, electromagnetism and the other fundamental forces found in the universe, but he never managed to prove it.)

While standing on the deck of a Victory class freighter, SS *Andrew Furuseth*, Allende said he witnessed the *Eldridge* literally disappear from the Philadelphia shipyard.

About 15 minutes later the ship reappeared. But, according to Allende, not without ill effect to the crew. His later investigations indicated many of the crewmen returned mad as hatters. Others were 'fused' (stuck) into the structure of the ship. Still others returned with a bizarre ailment: they drifted, uncontrollably and unpredictably in and out of our level of existence.

Where did the ship go for the 15 minutes it mysteriously disappeared? Allende told Jessup that witnesses in the port of Norfolk, Virginia, claimed it materialised there for a few minutes then vanished in a green fog. When Dr Jessup made Allende's claims public, they caused a sensation. Investigators rushed forward to check out the account ... and discovered a report in a local newspaper a few days after the ship re-materialized. According to the paper, two members of the *Eldridge's* crew got involved in a bar-room tussle. The barman called the Shore Patrol to restore peace, but before the officers arrived, both men vanished in mid-swing.

These are the bare bones of the story. But the Philadelphia Experiment – as the account is now known – has been retold, revised and elaborated on so often it's now almost impossible to find out the truth of the matter. Books, articles, a movie and several television documentaries have done little to shed light on what, if anything, Allende actually witnessed.

According to the US Naval and Maritime Service, neither the USS *Eldridge*, nor Allende's own ship, the SS *Andrew Furuseth*, was in Philadelphia on May 23, 1944, the date the incident supposedly took place. If neither the ship nor the witness were there, then the story is clearly nonsense. In short, the Navy meets any query about the Philadelphia Experiment with a flat denial.

A lot of investigators don't believe the Navy. They say that if the experiment was top secret to begin with, officials would have to deny it – particularly if it happened to be a success. They suggest it would be a small task to change ships' records in order to preserve the secret.

But would it?

The *Eldridge's* log indicates it was on convoy duty at the time. As a destroyer escort, herding and circling slower merchantmen, she was

observed daily by many other ships. Some of their logs would note her comings and goings during the course of the voyage.

On top of that, not a single member of the ship's crew ever came forward to tell the story of the destroyer's part in the legendary experiment or deny government evidence she was not in Philadelphia.

But the story doesn't end there. The US Department of Navy admits to an experiment that might have given birth to the legend. It involved a destroyer named the USS *Timmaron*.

The *Timmaron* was fitted with large electric generators and several pieces of equipment known as degaussers. Although Government sources remain tight-lipped about the details, it seems likely that the *Timmaron* was engaged in an experiment that did indeed involve Unified Field Theory but not to produce invisibility or teleportation, the two most popular myths about the Philadelphia Experiment. The US Navy claims the USS *Timmaron* was fitted with electronic equipment in an attempt to find out if it was possible to make a ship invisible to devices known as magnetic proximity fuses.

Before entering World War Two, the United States, had a very powerful secret weapon – the magnetic torpedo. This was a particularly deadly device. Because it used a ship's own magnetic field to detonate directly beneath the keel, it had several times more destructive power than torpedoes that exploded on impact. By the time the Philadelphia Experiment supposedly occurred, it had become obvious German submarines had a similar weapon.

While the magnetic torpedo remained secret until well after World War Two, the existence of magnetic mines was common knowledge throughout the conflict. Unlike contact mines, they did not have to touch the ship to detonate. Thus the Navy could well be telling the truth about the *Timmaron*. Any device that would help ships hide from magnetic mines or torpedoes would be of obvious benefit to the war effort; and the work of the *Timmaron* may have been based on Einstein's concept of a Unified Field Theory, exactly as the *Eldridge* was supposed to have been.

But there was one more factor that links the two ships. Where you have really large generators (of the type on board the *Timmaron*) you often get what are called coronal effects – an electrical field that builds up from small leakages in the equipment and creates a sort of halo effect around it. This halo would certainly explain the green haze Allende claimed to have seen around the ship he was watching.

Put all the pieces together and you have a logical explanation for the whole Philadelphia Experiment legend.

Or have you? There remains doubt that the Navy is telling the whole truth. While mines were certainly a threat to Allied shipping during World War Two, they were of minor concern compared to torpedoes. The numbers of ships lost to each type of weapon make this extremely clear. In the Atlantic, for every one lost to mines 20 were lost to torpedoes. If some device could defeat both, so much the better.

Making a ship invisible to a magnetic proximity fuse would certainly do the trick. If the ship's magnetic field could be eliminated, the torpedoes would speed beneath the surface until they ran out of fuel then sink harmlessly to the bottom. All the same, the method would be very expensive if it was intended to protect thousands of small freighters, each of which would have to be fitted with its own electronic array of magnetic invisibility equipment.

A more economic approach might be to suppose only warships, including destroyer escorts, were fitted with a different sort of electrical apparatus, one that projected a strong magnetic field some distance around the ship – a field strong enough to detonate magnetic proximity fuses 100 metres from their intended targets.

If this idea could be worked out technically, the destroyer escorts, ringing a convoy of merchant vessels, could protect the *entire group* from the threat of magnetic torpedoes. This would surely offer a more practical solution to the Navy's problem.

Whether the Navy's official version of magnetic invisibility or the more practical idea of field projection was the *Timmaron's* goal, it's possible the experiment accidentally stumbled onto an amazing discovery. What if the Timmaron's powerful electronic equipment produced an effect other than the one intended? What if it created the magnetic equivalent of a Black Hole? Most physicists suspect a connection between gravity and magnetism, so it may be possible – if only just – that the *Timmaron* accidentally opened a doorway to another world.

Incredibly, there are suggestions from the remote past that this may not be the only time humanity has deliberately tinkered with the locks between realities.

Chapter 12
Fairyland

Scientific statements about parallel worlds are relatively recent. Before the middle of the 20th century, science had nothing at all to say about them at all. But where science is silent, mythology often rushes in to fill the space. Interestingly, there is one myth that talks of people vanishing without trace while strange creatures sometimes cross over into the human world. This is the myth of a Fairy Kingdom that exists not quite on this Earth, but so close to it people – and fairies – can cross back and forth.

The most interesting thing about this myth is that it appears in almost every culture of the world, under one name or another. It's most widespread in Europe and Asia, less so in the Americas and Africa, but definitely present even there: and everywhere fairies share essentially the same characteristics.

The name *fairy* derives from the Latin *fatum* ('fate') and turned up in Middle English meaning 'enchantment' or, more often, 'a land where enchanted beings dwell'. The beings themselves at that time were referred to as *fays*.

Why the myth became so widespread is something of a mystery. Some authorities think it may have sprung up following the common experience of one tribe or nation conquering another. As the victors move in, the original inhabitants take to the hills and begin guerilla warfare. Since they attack stealthily by night, they seem supernatural.

Another theory is that the mythic fairies are a folk memory of an early pygmy race – an idea that has recently received some archaeological confirmation.

But none of the theories – and there are several others – actually account for every element of the fairy myth. One version, drawn from Irish folklore, is particularly interesting.

Parallel Worlds

According to traditional histories, original inhabitants of the country, known as the *Fir Bolg* were driven westward by invaders called the *Tuatha Dé Danaan*.

The *Fir Bolg* may have originated in Greece, but the *Tuatha* came from Heaven and supposedly landed their flying machines on the mountains of Connemara. They were followers of the Goddess Danu and were believed to be great magicians. With such a reputation, it's no surprise to learn that when the *Tuatha* were themselves supplanted by invading Milesians, they neither vacated the country nor died out, but rather installed themselves as a Fairy Kingdom within the country's 'hollow hills'.

As it happens, there really are hollow hills in Ireland: huge, man-made tumuli like Newgrange in County Meath into which rock-lined chambers and passageways were cut in prehistoric times. But legend has it that the *Tuatha* never lived inside the physical hills – the chambers are too small to accommodate more than a few dozen people at a time – but rather used them as a type of portal that allowed them to reach the Fairy Kingdom.

Throughout the world, the Fairy Kingdom is described as densely populated by a highly developed culture of creatures similar, but not identical, to humanity. The word 'kingdom' is possibly the wrong term, since the Fairy Realm is more often ruled by a Queen than a King. Its inhabitants enjoy fine food and good music and have a plentiful supply of precious metals like silver and gold.

Alongside the humanoid inhabitants, mythology speaks of tiny winged creatures and various more or less monstrous beings that have no similarity with anything in our own world.

So far the description of Fairyland is more or less what you'd expect from a traditional storyteller who set out to create a fairy tale. But there are three elements of the myth that are as odd as they are widespread.

The first is the conviction that time moves at a different speed in the Fairy Realm than it does on Earth. (In some versions of the myth, time ceases altogether.) The second is that it is possible, under certain circumstances, for human beings to enter Fairyland or fairies to cross into the human world. The third is that anyone entering the Fairy Realm is condemned to stay there forever if he or she eats fairy food.

You find these elements in folklore time and time again. The medieval poet, Thomas the Rhymer, was supposed to have gone 'over the river' with the Fairy Queen, but was able to return home safely because he declined all offers of food while in her realm.

Two Scots brothers were out and about one night when they noticed a light shining from a crevice in some rocks. They looked in to discover a company of fairies dancing. One brother went in to join them. When he failed to return for a year, the other brother protected himself with a Christian cross made from mountain ash and went into the hill. There he found his brother still dancing, convinced he'd only been away for a few minutes.

The time difference is even more dramatically highlighted in stories of humans who are permitted long-term stays in Fairyland, usually because they married a fairy man or woman. Legend after legend tells how, should the human decide to return to his own world, he discovers so many years have passed that his body ages instantly and he crumbles into dust.

Put the various elements together and you have an almost worldwide belief in a different dimension of reality, that is close to our own world but clearly not a part of it. In this parallel world, some of our familiar laws of physics no longer hold good, allowing actions that would appear magical to you and I.

In particular, the experience of time in the parallel world is quite different to that of our own, so that passage between the two worlds is dangerous. Nonetheless, the humanoid inhabitants of the parallel world are genetically so close to ourselves that interbreeding is actually possible – and has, in fact, taken place.

Time in the parallel world runs differently to time in our own. And anyone who mixes the atomic matter of the parallel dimension with his or her own by digesting food or drink, is locked into the different reality and unable to return to his own.

But all this, of course, is just a fairy tale. Isn't it?

Chapter 13
Real Fairies

In 1974, a Dutch couple visited Norway on holiday. Towards the end of their vacation, the wife went sightseeing on her own. She returned full of the news that she had seen a family of trolls camping by the roadside.

When her husband expressed disbelief, she could not understand his attitude. She was convinced that trolls were a near-extinct race of Scandinavian pygmies. Her husband had to show her the relevant entry in an encyclopedia before she would accept trolls as mythological creatures. But she continued to maintain she'd seen a family of them camped by the road.

At much the same time as this curious

incident, a retired civil servant living in Ireland reported an even more bewildering episode to one of his tenants. He was walking his dogs in a little wood on his estate when he came across a tiny man dressed in dull brown country clothing and sitting on a tree stump.

The creature looked so strange that the civil servant became excited and shouted at it in Irish. Hearing the commotion, his dogs – both terriers – came racing up barking furiously. He turned and shouted at them to keep away. When he turned back, the little man had vanished.

Only a few months previously, there was a further example of strangeness a short distance from the wood where the little man disappeared. This time the witness was not alone.

Jim Henry is a rally driver who runs his own motor mechanic business. In the early 1970s, he and his wife were visiting some friends who had recently moved into a remote country estate. The night of their visit was Halloween, a time when, by tradition, ghosts and spirits walk abroad.

Over the course of the evening, the conversation turned to matters weird and mysterious. Their host mentioned that on the estate, some distance from the house, was a prehistoric standing stone with a circular embankment of earth around it. This site, known locally as a rath or ringed fort, was believed to be the focus of all sorts of mysterious happenings. Years before, for example, an old woman out gathering firewood had broken some branches off a 'fairy thorn' (a blackthorn tree) near its entrance and was found lying dead on the spot the next morning.

Furthermore, cattle which grazed in the field surrounding the rath, never entered the rath itself. Some strange force seemed to keep them out.

Henry was intrigued and asked his host if he might visit this rath. The host agreed, but there was a problem. It was raining heavily that night and very dark. The rath lay more than a mile away, through a wood, over fields and across a stream. It would be difficult, if not impossible, to reach it unless the weather cleared. Around 11.20 p.m., it did.

Outside was bright moonlight with no more than a few scudding clouds. While the ground was soggy underfoot, the host said a visit to the rath was now possible.

Both the hostess and Julie Henry, Jim Henry's wife, decided not to go on the trip. Henry and his host dressed warm, pulled on wellington boots and set off at approximately 11.40 p.m. They reached the rath only a moment or two short of midnight.

The rath was set on high ground. Jim Henry and his host entered the earthwork ring through a gap in the structure near the fairy thorn which (according to legend) had killed the old woman.

Inside the ring, the ground sloped upwards like an inverted saucer, with the massive standing stone in the exact centre. Around the stone, about two metres distant from it, was a low metal fence put up when the site was excavated by archaeologists in the 1930s.

Henry's host remarked that there was an open cyst grave (a narrow slit-like burial place) immediately below the standing stone. The archaeologists had found ancient bones in it – of a woman and a wolfhound. Together they walked over to the fence and stood looking up at the stone. After a moment, Henry began to feel

distinctly uneasy. It seemed as if hidden eyes were watching him. The hair on the back of his neck began to prickle. It was, he knew, now midnight on Halloween.

'I don't think this place likes me,' he said.

'Do you want to leave?' his companion asked him.

Jim Henry nodded. The two men turned away from the standing stone and started to walk back towards the entrance. As they did so, a herd of about 25 tiny, pure-white horses, none larger than a spaniel dog, appeared at the top of the earthwork, galloped a distance of about twenty metres, then disappeared down the slope at the far side.

Henry and his host looked at one another, then broke into a run. They emerged from the earthwork only seconds later, but there was no sign of the tiny horses anywhere. They then climbed to the top of the earthwork and examined the soft ground with the aid of an electric torch. There were no hoofprints or marks of any sort.

The following day, the host made inquiries. He found there were neither horses, cattle nor sheep grazing in the area of the rath at that time. But he also discovered there were legends of 'fairy' horses associated with certain prehistoric sites. The stories insisted the beasts were white, much smaller than ordinary horses, and left no traces on the ground.

In the summer of 2004, the Jersey author Dolores Ashcroft-Nowicki paid a visit to Ireland and stayed for a week at my home in County Carlow. While she was there, she took several (digital) photographs of the walled garden. One was of a small wrought-iron gate.

When she returned to Jersey, she emailed a copy of the picture asking if there was anything to explain a small patch of light in the wall above the gate. Since the wall was solid, I could find no explanation other than a possible flare on the camera lens, But out of curiosity I enlarged the relevant area of the picture. When I did so, a faint but discernable winged female figure emerged.

What's going on here? So many countries worldwide have a folklore of 'fairies', 'elves' or 'little people' that experts think they may be memories of a wild Neolithic tribe, possibly pygmy, which had occasional shy contact with the developing Iron Age culture. But these modern-day accounts have nothing to do with long-dead pygmies. They describe strange happenings of historical times that continue to this day.

Although usually treated by the academic

establishment as a study of superstition and make-believe, folklore might equally be viewed as the recording of strange events that have kept occurring over time. While folk theory may be unsophisticated, this does not necessarily mean the original reports were inaccurate.

Viewed in this light, an exploration of fairy lore produces some interesting results.

First, there are several types of fairy folk and not all are the delicate little winged creatures that appear in children's tales or above my garden gate. William Allingham came closer to the reality of the matter when he wrote:

> *Up the airy mountain*
> *Down the rushy glen,*
> *We dare not go a-hunting,*
> *For fear of little men.*

The 'little men' of folklore often generate a fear reaction. Humanity, it seems, once learned to treat them with respect. Nor are the little men always little. In his *The Middle Kingdom*, folklorist Dermot MacManus makes the interesting point that a great deal of information on fairy folk can be discovered from law court records of the 16th and 17th centuries when the subject was taken far more seriously than it is today. Despite the fact that cases could arise as far apart as Scotland, France and Sweden, the fairies were invariably described as powerful beings living in organised communities under a local king and queen. They were often – McManus says usually – of human size or slightly larger and showed a handsome, dignified appearance.

In 1662, Isobel Gowdie, a well-educated Scotswoman, spoke of the King of Faerie as 'a brave man, well-favored and broad faced' when she met him in the Downie Hills. It is quite clear that Mistress Gowdie did not view the 'faerie' as any kind of spirit being since she claimed they'd given her more meat than she could eat. An intriguing detail of her story is the mention of 'elf bulls' bellowing and squealing, loudly enough to frighten her. What is being described here is something suspiciously like a small agricultural community.

Yet it is a community of individuals with unusual abilities. Historical accounts of the

French saint and martyr Joan of Arc concentrate on her mysterious voices and her claims of guidance from heaven, but at her actual trial there was much discussion of fairy folk. Here too it was clear that many, perhaps most, of the fairies were of human size, but the people of Joan's community, Domremy, were convinced they had 'powers over the destinies of men'.

Joan of Arc

They seem to have other powers as well. The late Colonel Henry Jordan, a member of an aristocratic Norman family, reported how one of the fairy folk (a little one this time) appeared suddenly in his daughter's bedroom when she was about six years old. The niece of Jordan's wife, an 18-year-old named Nora, also saw the creature, which was about 1.5 metres and standing about 2 metres from the child's cot. He disappeared as she looked at him.

Apart from his size and the fact that he was dressed in rather old-fashioned country clothing, the little man appeared perfectly normal until he vanished. He was clean-shaven, blue eyed and with light brown hair.

If this report was a dream or vision, it was a curiously persistent one for Nora saw him again three weeks later as the family were beginning dinner. Colonel Jordan also saw the creature at this time ... just before it disappeared again.

Months later, a workman on the Colonel's estate confirmed that he had seen the same – or very similar – figure in one of the fields when he was a boy; and like the Colonel, his niece and his child watched it disappear before his astonished eyes. When he told his fellow servants about the experience, a maid claimed she had seen the little man often.

The country Irish have never for a moment doubted the reality of fairy folk. To this day in the more remote areas, food – usually milk and soda bread – is left out for them, partly as a kindness, partly as a goodwill offering. The same practice is

followed in India and West Africa.

Yet despite their apparent solidity, the ability of the fairy folk to appear and disappear, apparently at will, is told in literally hundreds of stories. The only really unusual aspect of the Jordan case study is so many members of the Colonel's household witnessed the event.

But there is a significant aspect to certain of the disappearances, as seen by the following report of an incident that occurred at Longford, in Ireland, in 1932.

An 18-year-old servant girl, sitting on her day off beside a lake with some friends, heard the sound of horses on the road. She got up and told her friends she had better go back to the house where she worked as visitors were obviously coming and she would be needed to look after them.

She was running towards the house when the party of riders came into sight. There were eight of them, young men and women in bright clothing, laughing and talking among themselves. When they were little more than forty metres from the girl, they swung suddenly off the path to ride up over a grassy bank and across a field before riding casually into the side of a thorn-ringed 'fairy fort'. At this point the girl realized she was watching the activities of fairy folk.

There are interesting aspects to this report – aspects that appear again and again in many others. The first is that – at least up to a point – the visitors obeyed the laws of nature. Not only did they look and sound solid, but they rode up and over a grassy bank. They did not pass through it as, for example, a ghost might be expected to do.

But they were able to pass through solid matter 'as coolly and casually as humans would pass through a stable gate' at a certain point. They actually entered the side of another earthen bank a little further on.

Here we have the first indication that the mysterious appearances of the fairy folk may not be entirely random. The term 'fairy fort' used in this last report is identical to the term 'rath' in the story of the fairy horses involving Jim Henry. Both refer to a prehistoric ring fort. In the case of the fairy horse sighting, the ring fort surrounded a standing stone.

Even the briefest study of fairy folklore shows

a widespread connection between the fairy folk and megalithic sites. There are hundreds of stories of humans visiting such sites and being temporarily abducted into 'fairyland'. Even more stories tell of fairy revels (celebrations) seen at or around megalithic stone circles and ancient ring forts.

An equally strong tradition has it that the comings and goings of the fairy folk are along clearly defined paths, often forming a straight-line linkage between megalithic sites. The respected scholar and author, W.Y. Evans-Wentz was only one among many to suggest the paths are actually energy lines.

The suggestion has become fact throughout rural Ireland and other areas where belief in the fairy kingdom is strong. To this day, for example, it is possible to inspect a picturesque thatched cottage near Mount Nephin which has one corner neatly chopped off and rebuilt.

The cottage was originally constructed by a farmer named Patrick Baine as a home for himself and his wife. But when they moved in they were plagued by poltergeist activity so severe it seemed the house was in danger of falling down (poltergeists are invisible ghosts that move things around). The couple consulted a local expert who told them the trouble was that a corner of the house was interfering with a fairy path. A stonemason removed the corner and the poltergeist activity stopped at once.

The energy aspect of fairy appearance is further underlined by the dancing lights frequently associated with the sites, like the 'hundreds of twinkling lights like fireflies' seen spread across an area of ancient mounds between Kiltimagh and Bohola in County Mayo.

Sometimes this energy can have a very odd effect, described by the Irish term *foidin seachrain*. The literal translation – 'stray sod' – gives little clue to a phenomenon which appears not only in Ireland but in India, Africa and several other countries as well.

Briefly stated, *foidin seachrain* describes a situation in which an individual walking on familiar ground finds him or herself utterly lost and cannot find the way home. Dermot MacManus gives what he describes as 'two fully authenticated occurrences'.

In the first of these, which occurred in 1916, a County Leitrim rector named Harris was called out to visit a sick parishioner. He decided to take a short cut across a field which had fairy associations. The path, with which he was well familiar, entered the field through a large gate and left it again at the far side over a stile. The field itself was surrounded by a bank, topped by a thorn hedge.

Reverend Harris entered the field through the gate, walked towards the stile... and discovered it was no longer there. Nor when he looked down was the path. For two hours he searched for the stile, the path and even the gate through which he had entered. He could find none of them, although the field appeared in every other respect completely familiar. He had entered the field, but now something was stopping his getting out.

Then, for no apparent reason, something shifted. The gate, stile and path abruptly reappeared and the Reverend Harris was able to leave again. The date was Midsummer's Day, a time when fairy activity – and energies – is traditionally at a height.

The second of the MacManus reports is even more intriguing. It occurred in Mayo in 1935 and involved a 19-year-old girl who MacManus describes only by her initials, B. M.

Parallel Worlds

While walking to the home of some friends, the girl crossed a hill called *Lis Ard* which was surrounded by an ancient embankment. Although her environment looked perfectly familiar from the summit of the hill, when she went down to the gap in the outer bank something inexplicable occurred. She was jerked backwards and she found herself walking away from the bank and back towards a wood near the summit of the hill. She retraced her steps, but when she reached the gap, the same thing happened again.

By now thoroughly frightened, the girl then tried to climb over the embankment. To her horror she found herself stopped by an 'invisible wall'. She circled the entire earthwork. The force-

field surrounded it completely.

Night fell and still the girl could not leave the ring fort. She saw lanterns approaching and made out the figures of four men. She called out to them, then climbed onto the low bank, but though the men approached to within twenty metres it was quite clear they could neither see nor hear her. Two further search parties passed close to her with exactly the same result. She was watching a third disappear in the distance when she suddenly realized the invisible wall was no longer there and she was able to leave with no further difficulty.

A curious picture emerges from the folklore. It is a picture of ancient sites which produce energy phenomena like lights and force-fields and 'pulse' that energy along clearly defined tracks across the countryside.

This sort of statement reads like science fiction. But is it at all possible that our prehistoric ancestors knew more than we suspect about the reality of parallel worlds? Is it even possible that the great megalithic sites tourists visit today are the ruins of an ancient technology, a forgotten science, that opened portals into them?

Chapter 14
Megalithic Weirdness

There have been some very odd discoveries at megalithic sites in recent years. (Megalith means 'big stone'. A megalithic site is a prehistoric location that features big stones.) They were made not by archaeologists – although some archaeologists were involved – but by groups of individuals from both scientific and non-scientific backgrounds, bound together only by the belief that there were megalithic mysteries which went well beyond the usual ancient grave/ritual site type of explanation.

Two formal studies in particular have produced quite unpredictable results. One is the Dragon Project, founded in London in 1977. The other is

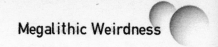

the somewhat more recent Gaia Program.

The studies examined megalithic sites throughout the British Isles. Preliminary results attracted the attention of a few academic establishments who were moved to supply specialist – and often expensive – scientific gear.

Over a period of years, Geiger counters (for measuring radioactivity), magnetometers (for measuring the strength and direction of a magnetic field), ultrasound detectors (to detect sounds beyond the range of human hearing), scintillation counters (for detecting and measuring radiation), electromagnetic field recorders, infra-red cameras and various other pieces of equipment have been used on megalithic sites. Some of the results have been startling.

In County Wicklow in Ireland, at the megalithic 'tombs' on Baltinglass Hill, radio signals emanate from the monuments, detectable in specific, clearly defined areas. Newgrange, in County Meath, by contrast, and one of the cairns at Loughcrew, have both exhibited the curious property of blanking out radio transmissions, including background noise.

Parallel Worlds

Elsewhere, ultrasound detectors operating in the broad 25–80kHz band have shown certain stones emit an ultrasonic click at sunrise and sunset, with a more generalised ultrasound pulse appearing intermittently at several sites.

Radiation readings at megalithic sites produced even more exciting – if somewhat bewildering – results. It has long been recognised that our environment is a sea of radiation, composed of energies from beyond the planet,[6] energies generated by the Earth itself (from, for example, radioactive decay) and various electromagnetic energies associated with human activity, such as radio and television broadcasting, electricity supply etc. This energy soup is known as background radiation.

There are some sites that give radiation readings higher than background and others, notably in Cornwall, where the readings are lower. This latter discovery is fascinating. It suggests that some stone circles act as a ring shield against radiation.

The effect is not subtle. Measurements taken in the summer of 1985 showed Geiger readings were actually halved by the shield. Three years

[6]Mainly but not exclusively solar.

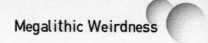

earlier, a steady drop in background radiation was noted at a site as a thunderstorm approached – the complete opposite of what you might expect.

At one circle, the Merry Maidens in Cornwall, measurements showed defined areas with above-background radiation levels, with neighbouring areas below background. Until the measurements were taken, such an effect was held to be impossible – and remains impossible to explain within current scientific theory.

In some instances, the effects associated with the megaliths have been so pronounced that they required no more delicate instrument than the human eye to record them. A stone in the western sector of the Rollright Stones in Oxfordshire showed dramatic short-term magnetic anomalies during a survey in 1983 and three years later produced a visible electric 'flame' which, while short-lived, was successfully photographed by investigator Paul Devereux.

There is already one solid linkage between these findings and a widespread folk belief. Several megalithic sites sport 'hole stones', aptly named megaliths with holes through which limbs and, in some instances, the whole body may be passed. According to folklore, passing someone through such a hole stone at the proper time can effect cures for various illnesses.

Rollright
Stones

Although this seems pure superstition, this belief has now taken on a whole new lease of life following the discovery that many megaliths generate an ultrasonic pulse at dawn. As any physiotherapist will confirm, ultrasound is effective in pain control, muscle spasm and speeding the healing of wounds. Electronic ultrasound generators now form a standard part of modern physiotherapy equipment.

But if the folk belief that certain megaliths were created as healing machines has now been

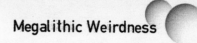

justified, how safe are we in dismissing the rest of the folklore? There are so many elements of these intriguing 'fairy stories' that point to a technology of other-world contact that it may be worthwhile investigating the great megalithic sites more thoroughly.

Chapter 15
Megalithic Machine

For years archaeologists underestimated how far back in time prehistoric man existed – almost as often as they underestimated his abilities. It was only with the invention of radiocarbon dating in 1949 (which uses radioactivity to measure the rate of decay) that the scientific community was forced to re-think the timetable of human existence.

At one point archaeologists dated Stonehenge, Newgrange in Ireland and other major megalithic structures as having been built around 1500 BC, 1,000 years after the Great Pyramid. This linked nicely with the theory that civilization started in the Middle East and spread outward.

Since the arrival of radiocarbon dating, we now know that the theory was unsound. Newgrange was built not in 1500 BC, but sometime earlier than 3300 BC – more than 1,000 years *before* the Great Pyramid.

Probably the most famous of all megalithic structures is Stonehenge on England's Salisbury Plain. It is one of thousands of megaliths spread throughout the British Isles, Europe, Asia and the Americas. (There are 50,000 dolmens in Europe alone – dolmens are tombs consisting of large stones – and the dolmen is only one type of megalithic monument.)

It is impossible to investigate the construction of Stonehenge without wondering what on earth our prehistoric ancestors were doing. These were the days before earth-moving machinery and diesel trucks. These were the days before Ancient Britons started to use horses. If you wanted earth or stone moved, you did it yourself with a group of your friends. It was immensely hard, back-breaking labour that required enormous time and trouble. Yet the people who lived on Salisbury Plain dedicated generations of labour to building something they were to tear

down and rebuild time after time. What drove them to do it?

Nearly 900 stone circles, or henges, have been identified in the British Isles. They range in size from Avebury, which circles a massive 11

hectares and has kilometres of twisting avenue leading to it, to the 2.5 metre high, quartz-studded leaning pillar in the centre of an isolated circle at Boscawen-Un in Cornwall.

Stone circles are also found throughout

Parallel Worlds

Western Europe, the Balkans, the Middle East, India, Tibet, China, the outback of Australia, the mountains of Peru, the jungles of the Yucatan, the desolate peaks of Wyoming and the hills of Ohio. The sheer volume of stone moved is mind-numbing. The capstone alone of Brown's Hill dolmen in Ireland weighs 100 tonnes. And nobody knows why our ancestors bothered.

But if circles are mysterious, standing stones are very, very mysterious.

Standing stones are often found in lonely fields far from any other monument or marker. But sometimes they appear in twos, threes and fours, in avenues miles long or close to other megalithic sites. Some are more than 6 metres high, others so short they're hidden in the weeds.

Many are nothing more than rocks moved into position. But some were shaped and smoothed before they were raised. Others have holes bored through them or their tops sculpted to match the horizon. Many are carved with primitive symbols. They can be found in nearly every country of the world.

Once again the question is why they were

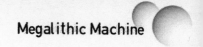

raised? Why did small groups of men involved in a day-to-day struggle for survival make the time to haul, work and lever thousands of kilos of stone into an upright position? And along with the question why, comes the question how. Wisdom has it that the stones were erected without the aid of levers, ropes, pulleys or even horse power. It was unaided human muscle, or unaided human inventiveness that put them up there, just as unaided human muscle and inventiveness moved hundreds of tonnes of earth to make artificial hills and other structures.

Tribes known as the Adena and later the Hopewell created over 10,000 earthen mounds in North America between 1000 BC and 400 BC. A few Native American tribes were still making mounds when the white man arrived but nothing as impressive as those built by their ancestors.

The Serpent Mound in south-central Ohio went undiscovered for many years. Although a hill of sorts was obvious from the ground, only from the air is it apparent that the mound's ridge is sculpted to form a giant serpent. In Newark, Ohio there exists one of several ringed mounds.

Again, seen from the air the mound forms a near perfect circle, encompassing over 9 hectares. Next to it an eight-sided mound rings 20 hectares.

Serpent Mound

Native American mounds come in all shapes and sizes, many bearing striking similarities to European barrows. Barrows are sprinkled over the countryside in such numbers that local residents take little notice of them. They are at least as ancient as the henges and standing stones, and were originally thought to be burial mounds. But excavation produced more doubts than evidence. Long barrows – mounds which are over 30 metres high and several hundred metres long – contained the remains of pitifully few people.

At first it was argued these were kings, but the theory falters when other, smaller grave sites are considered. These cairns and dolmens reveal bodies buried in a curled position and accompanied by prized possessions. In many barrows, which are large enough to contain thousand of skeletons, the position of the bones makes it evident that the bodies were thrown in helter-skelter – hardly the way a community would bury a revered member.

There are probably more mounds in China than any other country. Here they were often built in accordance with the ancient *feng shui* (pronounced 'fung sway') system which holds that shaping the countryside in certain ways will improve the luck and health of a site.

Closer to home, Glastonbury Tor, an artificially altered hill in Somerset is 158 metres at its highest point with a 304-metre whale-backed ridge running its length. Its steep sides are tiered with a maze. Crowned by St Michael's Tower, it dominates the landscape.

But as a work of early engineering, Glastonbury Tor, Ireland's hollow hills, or America's Serpent Mound are all dwarfed by structures known as cursuses, built, it is assumed, by the same peoples who built Stonehenge and the rest. The first cursus, discovered in the 18th century, was over 3 *kilometres* long, a linear earthwork that involved the movement of thousands of tonnes of earth.

Only nine more such earthworks had been discovered by the middle of the last century, suggesting they may have been very rare. But with the advent of aerial photography, it became clear that the cursus was a structure that was almost commonplace – the total discovered now is around fifty. One of them, in Dorset, is 9.6 kilometres long, covers an area of 89 hectares and contained, when built, an astounding 184,080 cubic metres of material.

Dorset cursus

Once again we find mound builders working on a worldwide scale. Based on available manpower estimates, it would have taken tribes months to finish even a small mound and many years for

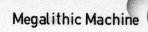
some of the larger examples. A cursus would probably have taken generations. Shifting 184,080 cubic metres of earth takes some doing.

Hill forts exist throughout the British Isles. Generally they comprise hills ringed with ditches and mounds and range in size from those too small to accommodate more than a few people to one in Dorset that has a 2 kilometre-and-a-half circumference enclosing 18 hectares. Many of these structures are referred to as contour forts because the ditches and mounds flow with the hill's natural formation.

Earliest hill forts date to 3500 BC and their excavations reveal they may have been misnamed. Because we look at these earthworks with 21st century eyes, it's often difficult to visualize their real use. Archaeological findings indicate they may have been ritual gathering sites rather than defensive settlements. Many of the largest contain no wells and there's little evidence to suggest a need for large scale defences before the Iron Age.

Yet in Scotland, the stone ramparts of several forts have been vitrified. Vitrification means heating stones until they become glass-like and flow into one another. The amount of heat needed is tremendous. Scientific attempts to duplicate the process using prehistoric technology have failed miserably. While a lightning bolt produces enough heat to fuse stone, it would require a continuous stream of lightning over a period of several minutes to duplicate what happened to the forts. Just one more mystery to add to the mounting total associated with the megalithic age.

Whatever the reason for the many huge monuments, it had to be important. We don't know much about the people who erected these structures, but we do know this: their lives were hard. Yet prehistoric man devoted generations of work to the megalithic sites. It is absurd to imagine his reasons were frivolous. He must have felt he had no choice but to undertake the labour and may have believed the survival of his species depended on how well he shaped the stones.

For us it will require an open mind, and a little more detective work, to discover why he did it.

Chapter 16
International Grid

Alfred Watkins was a prosperous merchant in Herefordshire. During the 1920s, he had sufficient leisure to become an enthusiastic amateur antiquarian (someone who studies ancient sites and artefacts), but an even greater love of his life was horseback riding. Most mornings and many weekends found him wandering with his pony across the picturesque countryside of the Bredwardine Hills.

On one such morning something very odd happened to Watkins. He had an intuition, amounting almost to a vision. It told him that various sites of antiquarian interest were aligned in straight lines. The idea seized him. He rode home furiously and opened up his Ordnance Survey maps. They showed his intuition was right. Many ancient sites really were lined up. And not just one or two – you could have as many as nine in a dead straight line.

To Watkins, there was nothing mysterious about these ley lines, as he came to call them. He thought they were the work of early travellers. But investigation soon began to shake Watkins' theories. He eventually came to believe he had been wrong about leys as trade routes, although some of them had certainly been used as general roads. The basic problem was that while a straight line may be the shortest distance between two points, it is not always the most convenient. Leys were dead straight. To follow them across country frequently presented travellers with obstacles that were almost insurmountable. The leys cheerfully crossed rivers, ravines and mountains, thick forests and soggy marshland.

But if leys did not mark what Watkins had called the old straight track, what did they mark? Investigators have made several interesting observations. One is that certain animals and

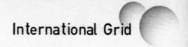

birds migrate along straight lines. Another is that the ley system is very ancient indeed. Although leys were sometimes marked by churches and castles, this seems to happen only when the buildings were erected on prehistoric sites. Watkins himself suspected a connection between the ley lines and the placement of ant hills.

The discovery of a British ley system – straight lines linking a variety of ancient sites – was quickly followed by the discovery of similar systems in Germany, France and the Middle East. But it soon became clear that leys were by no means confined to these areas. There are alignments in Belgium, Switzerland, Holland – indeed virtually every European country. Leys respect no national boundaries. Some run for hundreds of kilometres from country to country across the Continent. A few even cross from the British Isles into Europe.

There are indications that something very similar to leys exist throughout the United States, laid down by various native American cultures. In California, for example, early settlers found dead straight Miwok Indian trails linking cairns and shrines. Even more striking are the so-called 'Chacoan Roads' of New Mexico: hundreds of kilometres of dead straight trackways strung with monumental Great Houses erected by the Anasazi people.

These routes, built before the horse or the wheel were introduced into North America, were 9 metres wide and bordered by earthworks, dry stone walls or rows of stones. Thomas Sever of NASA (America's space agency), who investigated the network, is on record with the opinion that they linked specific places in the landscape rather than communities. In other words, they functioned not as roads, but as leys.

Mexico's Mayan culture built straight roads linking their sacred cities – at least one of them 128 kilometres (80 miles) long. The Incas of Peru were also noted for their sophisticated straight road system, reliably estimated to extend for 64,715 kilometres (40,220 miles). But the most interesting thing about Inca roads is that experts consider many of them follow an older system similar to European leys. These may have been associated with the ceques of Cuzco – alignments of sacred places identical to European leys.

Leys are also found in Australia, where they are

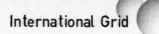

well known to the Aboriginal population. Different tribes look after different stretches of the lines (which they refer to as 'song lines') and travel along them performing appropriate religious ceremonies to activate them. Traditional diagrams known as *tjuringas* seem to be ley maps.

The idea that leys were ancient trackways has now been abandoned. But if not roads, then what? One answer arises from a curious source. British UFO investigators have noticed UFO sightings tended to clump close to ancient sites and the 'saucers' often fly in a straight line between them (i.e. along the ley). From these observations, a theory has grown up that the leys are actually lines of energy, a sort of power grid tapped by the extra-terrestrials to drive their vehicles.

Much the same idea – without the little green men – is mirrored in two very old traditions found at opposite ends of the Earth. In the more remote parts of Ireland there survives a belief in 'fairy paths'. These are tracks along which the little people move at specific, predictable times of the year.

As mentioned earlier, the Little People of Ireland are identified with the prehistoric *Tuatha Dé Danaan*, who are in turn closely associated with Ireland's megalithic sites. It comes as no surprise then to learn that fairy paths often lie along what Watkins called the ley lines. Folklore has it that when the paths are in use by the Little People, they are supposed to be particularly dangerous to humans. Anyone straying across them is in danger of being carried off by the fairy host or dying mysteriously.

There have been suggestions – in the works of W. Y. Evans-Wentz, for example – that the fairy path belief comes from an even earlier idea that some form of 'magnetic' force pulsed along the paths at regular intervals ... an identical idea to

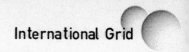

that held by modern UFO researchers.

Essentially the same concept appears in ancient China, where a complex system of sacred geometry includes the doctrine of the lung-mei, or 'dragon paths'. The study of sacred space in China is known as *feng shui*, a term literally translated as 'wind and water'.

Feng shui is based on the idea that all life is driven by a universal energy called *ch'i*, which is generated in the Sun. At the core of every *feng shui* calculation is the discovery of the Azure Dragon, a particular formation of the landscape that stores large quantities of *ch'i* and so acts as a power source.

The Dragon is thought of as the positive aspect of *ch'i* and cannot exist without its negative counterpart, referred to as the White Tiger. Here again, the Tiger is believed to hide in certain landscape formations.

A strong Dragon-Tiger combination creates a site with such a high concentration of *ch'i* that it might be called sacred. Interestingly, many of the megalithic sites of the West show features that would quickly be recognised by a *feng shui* expert from China.

Parallel Worlds

The *lung-mei,* or dragon paths, trace straight lines between the major sacred sites of China – areas where the *ch'i* has reached exceptional concentrations. They are thought of in China as representing an energy network that extends not just across the country, but over the entire face of the planet.

As in Ireland, Chinese belief held it was dangerous for humans to cross the *lung-mei* at those times when the energy pulse was at its peak. It was certainly dangerous to be buried on a *lung-mei* – that privilege was reserved for members of the Royal Family. Anybody who buried a commoner on a dragon line was put to death.

The idea that leys are energy tracks had curious implications. Since leys link sacred sites, energy is being carried to and from these sites. This means the sites themselves should no longer be considered in isolation, but rather be seen as cells in a larger network. What then is the network?

We are still a long way from answering that question, but a passage from the works of John Michel springs to mind.

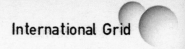

'We all live,' wrote Michel, 'within the ruins of an ancient structure, whose vast size has hitherto rendered it invisible. The entire surface of the earth is marked with the traces of a gigantic work of prehistoric engineering ... involving the use of polar magnetism together with another positive force related to solar energy.'

Michel suggests, in other words, that the megaliths and earthworks are the last remains of a gigantic prehistoric machine, powered by a network of energy lines much like the electricity network that criss-crosses our countryside today. From everything we have seen, it seems as if this machine may be somehow connected with the doorways to a parallel world.

Chapter 17
Here be Dragons

What are we to make of all this? Physicists tell us that parallel universes definitely exist. Folklore and myth describe other realities that have interacted with our own for centuries. To this day, things appear and disappear in ways that would suggest a two-way traffic involving some alien dimension.

But before we leave the present investigation, there is one chilling area that may repay closer attention...

Psychologists claim mythical monsters are creatures of the imagination, born in some nightmare mental realm, a symbol of humanity's need to face its fears. It's easy to see how this

could have come about. It's less easy to understand why different cultures throughout the world have created *exactly the same monsters*. Yet, if the psychologists are right, this is the bewildering situation that exists today.

Take one of the most famous monsters of all – the dragon. Dragons appear in the myths and histories of Europe and China, of the Australian Aborigines, of pre-Columbian South America, of the North American Indians Thunderbird and even the sacred records of Ancient Egypt. Is this some extraordinary coincidence of the imagination? Or could it possibly be an example of shared experience?

The earliest examples of dragons are found in the religious epics of two of our most ancient cultures. One is the Hindu *Rig Veda*, which celebrates the slaying of Vartra, a creature of cosmic menace. The second is the Babylonian legend of the Marduk who, using his own thunderbolt, slew the dragon Tiamat before 'light separated from darkness and time began'.

The *Rig Veda* is thought to have been written down around 1200 BC but only after the hymns from which it was composed had been sung for centuries. The story of Marduk slaying Tiamat appears in the *Enuma Elish* written around 1700 BC, but based on traditions earlier than 2000 BC. In her book, *British Dragons*, Jacqueline Simpson explains that these stories are concerned with the restoration of order after a threat of chaos.

The Mediterranean is particularly rich in dragon stories. Apep was the Egyptian dragon of darkness who pursued Ra across the heavens. The Greeks had Ladon, a multi-headed monstrosity that guarded golden apples bestowing god-like knowledge. They also recounted tales of their dragon, Typhon, the true son of chaos, a hundred-headed, fire-belching, rock-vomiting creature that caused storm and destruction wherever it went.

Moving north, we find similar beasts. The Norse god Thor baited a huge chain with the head of an ox to haul the gigantic Midgard serpent from the sea, only to have it escape as Odin, the father god, watched from the sky. There is also the classic tale of the dragon Fafnir, who guards the secrets of elfin gold. From France and the Alps come similar stories of dragons bested by local heroes.

The most famous dragon slayer of all is St

George. This courageous knight, always pictured with a Christian banner, galloped through stories all across Europe. So widespread was his legend that for centuries after his death he was claimed as the protector of England, Atalonia, Aragon, Italy and Greece and was revered from Lithuania to Portugal to Constantinople. His deeds include slaying dragons from Africa and Germany to Berkshire, England, where you can still find a place called Dragon Hill, made barren by the monster's venomous blood.

Despite the fantasy element so obvious in many of the myths, there are historians who believe George really lived. He was a martyr in Palestine sometime before AD 300, but beyond that, little else is known. The legend that he saved a Libyan princess by killing a dragon arose in the 12th century.

Even apart from Saint George, there is no

shortage of dragon tales in Western Europe. In England alone, over 70 villages and small towns have traditions of local dragons.

Dragon stories are even more widespread in the Far East. There are hundreds, perhaps thousands, of stories from China alone. Throughout Asia, dragons are represented as everything from brutal monsters to protectors of treasure, from bringers of storms to bringers of good fortune.

Across the Pacific, many stories in the New World centre around dragons. Among the North and South American Indians they were called by other names – firebird, thunderbird and winged serpents – but they remain recognisable.

In the Iroquois legend of a journey to Skyland, there are two dragons: the Great Blue Lizard known as Otkon and an enormous dragon-like serpent which, every so often, attempts to leave

its lair in the depths of the earth and destroy the surface inhabitants.

In the shimmering eeriness of the Northern Lights, the Yupik Eskimos still quietly speak of Tinmiukpuk, a huge fire-breathing bird which normally eats whales but sometimes, when angry, devours entire tribes of people, making you wonder briefly if this is what happened to the Eskimo village we mentioned earlier.

To the south, Aztec and Mayan histories yield up their dragons too. The god Quetzatcoatl, assumed the shape of a dragon-like creature to win his greatest battle and was often depicted as the 'precious serpent-bird'. The Aztec calendar shows a cipactic – part serpent, part crocodile – supporting the world on its back.

From the frozen Arctic to the Mayan jungles, from Europe's ancient forest to the burning sands of the Sudan, from the waters of the Yangtze to the Mississippi delta, you'll find stories of dragons.

Look at any culture's mythological creatures and you will find exaggerations of familiar animals. Until a few centuries ago, wolves ranged over a large part of the Earth. So it comes as no surprise to learn that wolves are found in myths. So are many other common animals like eagles, snakes, lizards, turtles and fish.

But while the hippopotamus is featured in traditional African myth, it never appears in Europe. In India and Persia, the tiger found its way into myth, but not elsewhere. Native American myths feature the coyote, but you'll look forever before you find that creature in the mythology of the British Isles.

Creators of myth have always tended to work with animals they actually knew. Sometimes several different creatures were combined to create monstrosities with awesome powers, but they always originated in the experience of the storyteller. So what was it the storytellers experienced that gave rise to dragon myths?

Dragons are not unique as universal mythical creatures. Demons, gargoyles and creatures from spirit worlds all appear throughout the world. As just two examples of this wide-ranging breed, I might spoil your sleep tonight by examining just two – shape shifters and vampires.

It is difficult to deal with either of these subjects. While they appear in very ancient myths, they have been treated so sensationally in literature and movies that it's nearly impossible to separate the genuine legends from their Hollywood versions. There are over 100 English-speaking films featuring vampires which have combined to create an entire lore of the undead that has little to do with the original stories.

To understand the vampire's basis in folklore, you have to forget the Hollywood image of a slick, sophisticated, sinister seducer. If a real vampire appeared on your doorstep, he or she (and they're just as likely to be women) would probably be of stout peasant stock with long, thick fingernails. The ruddy, swollen face might present an open left eye and gaping, drooling, mouth. The attire for the evening would most likely be filthy, shabby clothes, or maybe even a burial shroud. It's a long way from the Eastern European nobility of Count Dracula.

In fact, the image is closer to that of a ghoul. The reason for this is ghouls and vampires are more or less interchangeable in many countries. Both drink blood and eat the flesh of humans. In North and South American Indian myth, they are sometimes referred to by names that loosely translate as 'undead cannibals'.

In Europe alone there are over twenty supposed vampire species. From the *Nachtzeher* of Bavaria to the *Bruxsa* of Portugal to Ireland's *Dearg-dul* they each possess distinctive traits.

It is a widely held belief that vampire legends began in Eastern Europe and spread outward, but this is not the case. The earliest written accounts of vampire myths are found in Babylonia and Assyria. The Babylonian vampire, or *Ekimmu*, was a spirit that travelled until it found a luckless man who 'had wandered far from his fellows into haunted places'. It then fastened on the poor mortal, making him behave in a gruesome fashion. A Babylonian inscription on a stone tablet bears this verse about *Ekimmu*:

Knowing no mercy,
They rage against mankind:

They spill their blood like rain,
Devouring their flesh and sucking their veins.

Southern Greek vampires, sometimes known as *Bucolacs* or *Vrykolaka*, are as old as the stories of their ancient gods. Many Greeks believed the creature wasn't really a dead human somehow revived, but an evil spirit which entered the body after its owner has withdrawn.

In Northern Greece the vampire was called a *Vrukolaka* and there too it was believed to be a devil that entered a body, making it rise from the grave to wreak havoc in the village. Vampires were called *Katakhanas* in Crete where an ancient legend claims one was seen gnawing on a human liver.

Even in England, the home of the fictional vampire, we find legends dating from the 12th century that have the creatures feasting on corpses at fresh graves.

India has a wide range of *vampiric* monsters. The form known as *Panangglan* is more or less a normal blood-sucking type, but the *Jigar-Khor* follows a feast of blood with a dessert of liver.

In the Tamil *Dream of Harichanda* a strange little man named Sandramati claims to be a *Vetala*, a race of elves which feed on children's flesh.

Another Far Eastern vampire is the mysterious *Mati-anak*, a weird little white animal that makes noises around graves. In Hindu myth, Siva is identified with *Mrityu*, Death, and his old name *Pacupati*, Lord of Herds, acquired the chilling meaning of 'Master of Human Cattle'.

Vampires are no strangers to Australia. During the night following a death, Aborigines will sit round the body, chanting to prevent the evil spirit from taking it away. The Arabs and Persians have pre-Christian myths about vampires, which are also known as ghouls and lamias.

In the book of Isaiah in the Bible, chapter 34, verse 14, there is a prophecy foretelling Babylon's ruin. According to the readings of an early popular Bible, Babylon would become the home of *lamias* and *strygie* (another name for vampire).

If there was a place on Earth where vampires were more abundant than Europe, it was China. Here, where they are called *kiangshi* (corpse-spectre), the methods for destroying them were written down and passed religiously from one generation of village headman to the next.

The Incas, Aztec and Mayan cultures usually referred to their vampires as cannibal spirits or

vampire devils. Even today, the Amazon is still alive with tales of recent encounters with jungle ghouls.

North American Indians did not lack vampire lore. But their monsters were as much cannibal as blood-drinker.

One fascinating tale comes from the Cherokees. *Nunyunuwi*, the Stone Man, walked the woods alone, carrying a cane made of quartz. Occasionally he would stop, point the cane in a direction then smell its tip. He would repeat the process until he smelled humans, at which point he would move in that direction.

In the legend he was very difficult to kill. Finally, a medicine man tricked him and ended his reign of terror by driving wooden stakes through his body.

The vampire, by any of its names, is unquestionably one of the most widespread myths in the world. Another is the myth of the shape shifter. There is simply no known culture that does not have its werewolf, werefox, wereleopard, weretiger, weresnake or even werehare.

Legends of people turning into fierce animals, killing and devouring victims, are even more abundant than vampire stories. One tells how, in 1584, a werewolf attacked a small girl in a village in the Jura Mountains. When the child's brother came to her aid, the werewolf killed the boy. Villagers attacked and clubbed the creature to death ... and, to a man, reported seeing the beast turn into a young woman.

Creatures like demons, dragons, shape shifters and the rest have no place in our natural ecology. If they did, biology would long since have charted them. Worldwide mythology claims some of them at least – demons and spirits – originate in a different level of reality.

If this is so, perhaps John Michel's 'megalithic machine' wasn't so much meant to open portals to another world as to keep them closed.

Afterword

This has been the most speculative of all my Forbidden Truths books so far. Where the evidence presented in the first three titles seem to me to point in only one direction, the evidence presented in this one really points towards a mystery. So what can we really say for sure about parallel worlds?

The first thing we can say is that they definitely exist. Einstein's work has shown this conclusively. It is also safe to say that portals into parallel dimensions lurk in the forbidden depths of Black Holes.

Are there more accessible gateways? The honest answer is we don't know, but case studies and legends like those of a Fairy Kingdom all suggest there is two-way traffic between the worlds right here on Earth. For centuries, this traffic has been closely associated with megalithic sites constructed worldwide in prehistoric times.

Parallel Worlds

Once we go beyond that, we are on far less certain ground. Are megalithic sites the remnant of an ancient technology lost to modern science? Is there a hidden energy grid that powers the great stones? Do the megaliths themselves form a sprawling machine of almost unimaginable proportions designed to give us entry into other worlds ... or keep Otherworld inhabitants out?

The plain fact is no one knows the answer to these questions. When it comes to these forbidden truths, you will have to make up your own mind.

Index

Allingham, William 143
Ansbach 9, 20
Avebury 162
Azure Dragon 177

Barrows 166
Bathurst, Sir Benjamin 78–81
Black Holes 105–110, 118, 193
Bermuda Triangle 70–76
brimstone 38

ceques 174
Chacoan Roads 174
cursus 167–168
cyst grave 138

Daumer, Georg Friedrich 20, 22
Dei Gratia 93
Devil's Triangle 75–76
Devonshire Devil 58
dolmen 161, 164, 166
Dracula 187
dragon paths 177–178
Dragon Project 154

Einstein, Albert 103–110, 118, 120, 193
Eldridge, USS 119–123, 125
escape velocity 107
Evans-Wentz, W. Y. 149, 176

Everett, Hugh 117
extra–terrestials 176

fairy horses 140, 148
fairy paths 176
feng shui 167, 177
fish, falling 44–47, 49
foidin seachrain 150
frogs, falling 47–50, 52–54

Gaia program 155
Glastonbury Tor 167
Great Pyramid 160–161

hailstones 36, 47
Hauser, Kaspar 9–23, 26–28
Hesperus 96
hill forts 169
hole stones 157–158

ice, falling 34–38, 42
Iron Mountain 67–70
islands, disappearing 76–78

Joan of Arc 145

Kerr, Roy P. 110
Kobenhaven 69

Leichhardt, Ludwig 97
ley lines 172–176, 178
Magonia 41–42

Manila vampire 61
Mary Celeste 92–95
Michel, John 178–179, 192
Mothmen 61

NASA 174
neutron star 107
Newgrange 160–161
Nuremberg 10, 16

OOOPs (Objects Out Of Place) 42

Pewt ser 37
Pickering USS 71
poltergeists 149–150
polypropylene 37
probability waves 116–117
pygmy 129, 135, 142

Ralph of Coggeshall 30
Rig Veda 181
Rollright Stones 157–158

Quantum Mechanics 111

Serpent Mound 165–167
shape shifters 186, 191–192
song lines 175
St George 182–183
standing stones 137–139, 148, 164
Stonehenge 102, 160–163

Theory of Relativity 104–106, 111
Thomas the Rhymer 132
Timmaron, USS 124–125, 127
tjuringas 175
Tuatha Dé Danaan 130, 176

UFO 175, 177
Unified Field Theory 120, 124–125
Unlucky Ninth 98–99

vampires 186–192
vitrification 169

werewolf 191–192
Wessenig, Captain 11–14
White Tiger 177
William of Newburgh 30
Woolpit 23, 27–32
Wüst, Sergeant 14–15